Jungle Princess

Holly Copella

In loving memory of
Donny & Alice Morris

ACKNOWLEDGMENTS

Copella Books: First Paperback Edition 2018
Printed by CreateSpace, An Amazon.com Company
Cover Artist: Daniela Owergoor
Dani-owergoor.deviantart.com

PUBLISHER'S NOTE

Chapter One

The five-hundred-passenger cruise yacht sailed across the ocean just after sunset in the early evening. Clouds rolled in with the approaching storm as the ocean became harsh and unruly. The passengers would be in for a massive storm later that night, although none seemed to give it a second thought. Most of the passengers just went about their evening plans. The elegant dining room was filled with well-dressed men and women at first seating having dinner. The dining room held a little over two hundred passengers seated at round, four-person tables with a candle centerpiece. Fine china and crystal glasses added to the ritzy atmosphere.

An attractive woman in her late thirties, Trisha Knight, dined with her boyfriend, Bronson Sharp, and her fifteen-year-old niece, Alexis Knight. Despite being a teenager, Alex looked like a young woman in her early twenties. She was often mistaken for a college student. Her girl-next-door good looks caught plenty of attention, although she wasn't interested in boys at the moment. She wore a short, black evening dress with the hem reaching just above her knees.

Alex wasn't a fan of high heels, but she was prompted to wear them to dress up for dinner. She'd actually borrowed them from her aunt, who wouldn't allow her to wear her boots with the dress. She wore her long, dark hair down despite the urging for her to wear it up in a similar style as her aunt. She knew her aunt was trying to create memories for them of their first official trip together as a family. Alex appeared bored and poked at her artistic meal.

"So, Alex, what are your plans for this evening?" her Aunt Trisha asked.

"I suppose I'll just hang out at the under twenty-one club," Alex replied with little emotion. "There's not much else to do on this cruise."

"There's plenty to do, you're just not participating," her aunt insisted.

Alex's Aunt Trisha shared many of Alex's features and could almost pass for Alex's older sister. That she looked similar to Alex's mother was both comforting and troubling. Trisha had the same dark hair as Alex, although she wore her shoulder length hair up in a French twist. Trisha wore an expensive sapphire blue dress that fell below her knees and showed plenty of leg and cleavage. Maybe the dress was just as much for her boyfriend as it was for the expensive meal. Alex had mixed feelings about her Aunt Trisha's boyfriend.

Bronson was a fairly good-looking man in his mid-thirties. He had perfectly styled, light brown hair that nearly touched his shirt collar. He was a moderately muscular man and looked fine in his expensive suit. The fact that Bronson couldn't anymore afford the suit than the cruise immediately set the tone for his relationship with her aunt. She always felt Bronson was a gold-digger, but if her aunt didn't seem to mind, it wasn't Alex's place to point it out.

"I'm not much for shuffleboard with the old folks," Alex announced while looking bored. "There's hardly anyone under twenty on this entire ship."

Trisha shifted uncomfortably and managed a timid smile. "I had hoped you'd be able to make some new friends onboard."

"I guess I lost all of them when I lost my mom and dad," she replied without looking up.

Trisha tensed then eyed Bronson.

The handsome man immediately took his cue. "I'm going to the little boy's room," he announced then left the table.

Trisha moved her chair closer to Alex and stared at her with a sympathetic look. "I know this hasn't been easy for you, Alex, but you and I are going to get through this," she assured her while placing her hand on her lower arm. "You'll make new friends at your new school."

"I know you're trying, Aunt Trish," Alex replied and finally looked into her eyes. "I just need time to be miserable."

"Of course," Trisha replied then straightened. "Look, I want you to enjoy yourself this week. Go flirt with some boys. You're not having any fun hanging out with us." She waved her off while offering a moderately devious grin. "Go. No curfew tonight, okay?"

Alex appeared surprised then smiled more naturally for the first time. "Thanks, Aunt Trish."

She kissed her aunt on the cheek then left the table. Bronson stood near the bar, watched her leave, and then returned to the table.

"Let the girl off her leash?" he teased.

"She's going through a lot right now," Trisha remarked then sighed seeming defeated. "The girl deserves a little fun."

Chapter Two

Alex walked along the brightly lit deck as the night wind whipped. She watched passengers rush to their destination, knowing most of them feared they'd sacrifice their carefully styled hair if they didn't hurry back inside. It was all about prestige and presentation for the wealthy passengers onboard the first-class cruise yacht. She couldn't fault her aunt for being wealthy and choosing this particular cruise. Her aunt wanted to show her a good time, and expensive, first-class vacations were her idea of a good time. No one told Aunt Trisha it wasn't really the scene for a young teenage girl.

Alex stopped by the railing near an isolated section of deck and looked at the dark ocean while tears streaked her face. She attempted to push the death of her parents from her mind for her aunt's sake, but she couldn't keep up her cheerful appearance. The approaching storm matched her mood, and the rumbling thunder didn't mind if she showed her emotions. As she stared at the violent storm off in the distance and the choppy water they sailed through with little incident, Alex removed her shoes and stepped onto the lower rung. Alex wasn't sure what was going through her mind at that moment, but she knew she couldn't handle the desperation and despair she was unable to shake. She just wanted to be free from her dark emotions.

"Careful, you might fall in," came a male voice from nearby, which startled her.

Alex jumped off the rail and looked behind her into the dimly lit area practically hidden beneath the stairs. A neatly dressed man in his late forties sat at one of the small tables obscured by the shadows. Although he was dressed in what appeared to be an expensive suit, he looked more like a high school chemistry teacher without the bowtie. He held a glass of champagne in his hand while the expensive bottle of bubbly set on the table near an empty second glass. She was genuinely surprised to see someone sitting in such a secluded area alone, but she didn't let it show.

"I'm not that lucky," Alex remarked under her breath while turning to face him.

"You and me both, kid," Holt muttered then sipped his champagne while staring blankly at the ocean.

Alex eyed him suspiciously, slipped into her shoes, and then approached him. "Are you okay?"

"I'm coping," he announced then grinned playfully. "Thanks for asking."

Alex indicated the empty glass on the small table. "Did your friend miss the boat?"

"No, no one missed the boat," Holt replied while maintaining his smile and seemed oddly cheerful. "I'm celebrating my twenty-fifth wedding anniversary."

Alex tilted her head with a bewildered look. He refilled his glass, hesitated, and then filled the second glass.

He eyed Alex then indicated the glass. She sat in the empty seat.

"Where's your wife?" she finally asked.

Holt sighed. "Dead," he replied with a sedate look as he seemingly stared through her. "Brain aneurysm." His eyes met hers. "She went to sleep and never woke up."

Alex stared at him while feeling the tears welling in her eyes. "I'm sorry."

He studied her a moment then tilted his head with great interest. "I'm guessing you're upset about something more than my wife's passing."

She tensed slightly and avoided looking at the mildly drunken man. "My parents died last month in a car accident," Alex replied softly. "My aunt and her ill-conceived boyfriend thought this cruise would cheer me up."

There was an awkward silence.

"I'm sorry, dear," Holt replied timidly with understanding then drew a deep breath. "Sometimes we just want to be sad." He then offered a tiny, drunken smile and raised his glass to her. "To your parents."

Alex picked up the glass and gently clinked it to his. She always wanted to clink glasses as they did in the movies.

"To your wife," she announced.

Both sipped the champagne. Alex made a face at the taste and nearly gagged as the bubbles went up her nose.

"It's expensive champagne," Holt informed her with a humored grin on his face. "Ironically, the hangover is going to feel exactly the same as the cheap stuff." He studied her a moment. "What's your name?"

"Alex."

"It's a pleasure to meet you, Alex," he replied in a refined tone. "I'm Holt." He watched her a moment longer then chuckled. "You must be bored out of your mind. Not exactly the college party scene you're used to, huh?"

"I wouldn't know," she replied simply. "I start high school next year."

Holt's expression dropped as he stared at her. "High school?" he practically gasped. "How old are you?"

"Fifteen."

He looked away and hid his smile. "If anyone asks, you didn't get the alcohol from me."

Almost an hour later, Alex and Holt stood at the railing despite the approaching storm and finished the last of the champagne. Holt threw his glass into the ocean then looked at Alex. She smiled and did the same.

"Thank you, Alex," Holt announced cheerfully. "I feel oddly better than I thought I would tonight."

"Yeah, me too," she replied then giggled for reasons unknown. "I'm tingly all over."

"That's because you're drunk," he teased, "but that'll be our little secret."

"I totally agree," she informed him. "I don't think my aunt would be very understanding if she found out."

"And I'd be in serious trouble for providing the alcohol in the first place," he replied.

Although she didn't know what time it was, she was certain it was getting late. "I should probably go," she announced, enjoying the tinglies throughout her body. "Goodnight, Holt." She then kissed him warmly on the cheek.

Holt hid his boyish grin. "Goodnight, dear."

Chapter Three

Club Teen resembled most popular city dance clubs with a large dance floor, dim lighting, and a DJ playing the latest, hip, modern music loud enough to drown out every last voice. It was also the only place onboard where those under twenty-one could have any real fun. Since there was no alcohol served, parents knew it was a safe haven for their teenage children.

Most of the ship was designed for adults over twenty-one or little kids under twelve, leaving little excitement for anyone under the legal drinking age. Alex danced with a group of teenagers possibly older than herself, but since she looked older than her actual age, she fit in with them. The club was packed with young patrons, although many were clearly over twenty-one.

Compared to the other club goers, Alex was slightly overdressed. Only a few young women wore dresses and most were much shorter than hers and revealed far more cleavage. Despite that Alex thought the music was too loud and prevented her from talking to the girls she danced with, it also kept her from thinking about the wreck her life had become seemingly overnight. She was able to keep the death of her parents out of her mind even if it was just for one evening.

§

It was nearly 2:00 A.M., and the storm was raging outside the ship. Lightning flashed and thunder cracked while waves struck the ship, rocking it despite its size. Passengers could feel the gentle rocking, but it wasn't enough to disrupt their evening, and a large portion had already turned in for the night. The wind whipped harshly, seemingly blowing in every direction while the rain poured down.

Once Club Teen officially closed for the night, Alex left the club and hurried along deck with her new friends. The brief moments they'd spent on deck were enough to soak the group of teens. When they finally reached the interior corridor, they were able to laugh at their soaked condition. Alex was lucky she was able to run in the dress shoes her aunt insisted she wear. Her new friends saw her safely to her cabin before heading to theirs, which was another deck away.

Alex entered her cabin and turned on the light. Her cabin was rather luxurious for someone her age. It had a full-size bed with all the frills, a private, full-sized bath, and a large ocean view window. Alex immediately kicked off her wet, uncomfortable dress shoes. She'd have blisters after dancing in them all night. She grabbed a towel and immediately started drying her hair. She knew she should take a shower before going to bed, but it was already late, and she didn't have the energy.

Alex tapped lightly on the connecting door to her aunt's cabin, wanting to let her know she had returned from her evening out so she wouldn't worry. There was no response. She hesitated, fearful she might see something she didn't want to see and then opened the door to the dark connecting room.

"Aunt Trish?"

Her aunt's cabin was dark and empty. She realized no curfew also meant her aunt and Bronson could party all night as well. She shut the connecting door and headed for the bathroom to slip out of her wet dress when the ship suddenly rocked. A harsh vibration was felt throughout the entire ship. Alex was thrown against the wall with tremendous force, knocking her to the floor. She was slightly stunned but quickly moved to her feet, wondering what had happened.

The ship's alarm wailed loudly, sending panic through her. Despite her alarm, Alex was able to keep her wits about her. She slipped into her black boots, grabbed her life preserver, and hurried from the room. As she ran along the corridor, she realized she was running on a downward incline. People filtered out of their cabins and into the corridor, panicking when they saw the angle of the corridor.

Chapter Four

Crowds of people pushed into the once glamorous, ritzy lobby. Its tall interior ceiling that led to several interior cabins on multiple levels and polished brass and glass staircase was no longer the prime focus. Throngs of people pushed and shoved one another despite the crewmembers attempting to keep them calm while awaiting further orders.

Word had already spread that lifeboats were being filled as a precaution, but most knew it wasn't a precaution. They realized the ship was sinking. It wasn't long before smoke filled the lobby causing more panic to ensue. Alex entered the lobby and was immediately shoved against a wall as people pushed past her. She stood near the wall, attempting to keep from being trampled while watching the crowd of once refined, wealthy people reduced to a mob mentality and every man for himself.

The crewmembers attempted to direct the masses to the exit doors since the smoke was now getting heavy, clouding the tall ceiling and lowering visibility. Directing more people onto the lifeboat decks in the severe weather wasn't ideal, but it was now the only option remaining. Unfortunately, most of the passengers no longer listened to the frantically shouting crewmembers but instead pushed and shoved their way to the nearest exit.

Alex witnessed a young woman tumble down the elegant stairs while being pushed within a crowd only to have that same crowd trample her at the bottom. Alex remained pressed against the wall with fear sweeping through her as she surveyed the situation from a safe distance. She knew she had to get to deck, but she also needed to find her Aunt Trisha. She continued to scan the crowd, hoping to catch a glimpse of her aunt, since the lobby was the designated meeting place. Still, she didn't see any sign of Trisha.

Bronson appeared within the crowd, saw Alex against the wall, and pushed his way toward her. He grabbed her arm to keep her from being pushed aside by the panicking masses.

"Are you okay?" he practically cried out, obviously losing his rational thinking along with the mob.

"Yeah, I think so," she announced while attempting to catch her breath as she watched the herds of people pushing and shoving one another through the smoke-filled lobby. She looked back at Bronson. "Where's Aunt Trish? She wasn't in the room."

"I left her in the lounge when I went to the casino," he announced while scanning the crowd. "She's probably already on deck with everyone else." His eyes then met hers with a serious look. "The ship's sinking, Alex. We need to reach the lifeboats."

He wasn't telling her anything she hadn't already suspected, but hearing him confirm it caused her heart to pound. Bronson took Alex's arm and pulled her behind him as he followed the crowd attempting to get out of the smoke-filled lobby. Passengers clogged the opening leading onto the deck. With all their pushing and shoving, few were able to make it through the doorway. A frantic crewmember continued to shout orders at the people who ignored him.

"Use the aft doors," he cried out while motioning to another set of doors on the opposite side of the lobby. "Use the aft doors!"

Alex saw the cleared doors across the lobby and pulled on Bronson. "This way!"

Bronson hesitated at first then followed Alex to the aft doors that were virtually wide open. Alex and Bronson hurried into the nearly empty corridor. The aft deck was to the left, and the lounge was to the right. Alex hurried to the right.

Bronson appeared surprised by her sudden direction change and pulled on her wrist. "Alex, the deck is this way!"

"We have to check the lounge for Aunt Trish," she shouted back while pulling on his hand firmly gripping her wrist.

Alex broke free from his grip and hurried for the lounge. Bronson frowned, shook his head, and headed for the deck with the others. Alex hurried into the empty lounge. To her horror, the entire back wall was smoldering and billowing smoke, although the smoke still hadn't reached the front portion of the lounge. She turned to leave when she saw Holt sitting alone at the bar. He casually drank a glass of expensive brandy with the bottle on the bar in front of him.

"Holt--?"

He turned his head and stared at her with some surprise. "Alex? What are you doing here?" he casually asked. "Didn't you hear? The ship is sinking."

"Yeah, so why are you still here?" she demanded and hurried toward him.

He shrugged and offered a drunken grin. "Laws of physics, human nature, mother nature. Add them together, and there's no scenario where this ends well," he replied. "I've accepted my fate. I have nothing left to fight for." Holt took her hand, kissed it warmly while grinning, and indicated the door in a grand gesture. "Go, Alex. Fight for life."

Alex appeared surprised while staring at him. He released her hand and, without a care in the world, refilled his brandy glass. Alex stared at him only a moment longer then sat on the stool alongside him.

"What do I have to fight for?" she suddenly asked while staring at him.

"You have your entire life ahead of you," Holt insisted in his drunken tone. "You have everything to live for, my dear."

"My life is no more valuable than yours," she informed him. "Everything I've ever had is gone. My parents, my home, my friends. I have nothing but an aunt who doesn't need to be burdened with a teenager." She stared at him through eyes void of life. "My will to live died in that car with my parents."

Holt stared at her with a moderately stunned look. Alex took the glass from him and drank the entire contents in one gulp. She gagged on the substance and immediately made a face.

"Oh, that's nasty."

Alex reached for the bottle. Holt caught her wrist without taking his eyes off her. His look was surprisingly serious.

"You need to get off this ship," he practically ordered. His jovial mood was stern. "Now."

"Not without you."

Holt looked at the fire across the lounge with realization of their situation. He jumped off his bar stool while pulling Alex behind him and headed for the lounge door.

Chapter Five

Nearly two hundred people crowded the deck on the aft side of the ship, which meant there had to be over three hundred on the port side. The crew attempted to keep the passengers calm while boarding the lifeboats despite the rapidly sinking bow. The lifeboats weren't very stable in the violently churning waves, making loading them chaotic and frightening. The fire was now reduced to billowing smoke, which caused more panic for the frightened passengers.

The raging storm pounded them with rain and wind. The heavy waves crashed against the ship, making it nearly impossible to load the lifeboats safely. People pushed and shoved one another while several fights erupted among well-bred gentlemen. Bronson pushed his way along deck, attempting to get closer to the lifeboats.

"Bronson," Trisha could be heard crying out from somewhere on deck.

Bronson looked around and saw Trisha rapidly being pushed further away from the lifeboats by the panic-stricken passengers. He fought his way through the crowd to reach her, but he wasn't getting any closer.

"Where's Alex?" she cried out from across the deck. "Did you see Alex?"

Bronson hesitated only a moment and shook his head. "No, I didn't see her," he called back. "Maybe she made it to the port side lifeboats."

Trisha attempted to push her way closer to Bronson while clutching the deck railing. Wind and rain continued to soak the passengers as the ship rested on a hard angle. A fight erupted near Trisha. Two men punched each other for unknown reasons. Their situation was already turning into every man for himself. One man was thrown against Trisha, and she was catapulted over the railing, screaming as she plummeted into the choppy water. She screamed to Bronson. He leaned over the railing and watched her while her life preserver kept her afloat.

"Don't panic," he called to her over the railing. "I'll get you out!"

"Hurry!"

Trisha attempted to swim closer to the boat, but the choppy water left her floundering. Bronson ran his fingers through his wet hair then saw a lifeboat near him being prepped. He glanced at Trisha over the railing then looked back at the lifeboat. He abandoned his crusade to help Trisha and pushed past several men and women to reach the lifeboat. A man placed a hand on his wet jacket and stopped him from reaching his destination.

"Where do you think you're going?" the angry, soaking wet man suddenly demanded and shoved Bronson back a step. "Women and children first."

Bronson punched the man and shoved him aside.   A fight broke out as several men attempted to stop Bronson from boarding the lifeboat.

Chapter Six

Holt and Alex appeared on deck within the mass chaos. Holt grabbed her arm and pulled her back just in time to avoid a scuffle between two men. Alex was stunned at the behavior of supposedly rational people. Both watched in horror as several people fell overboard by accident and others with a little help. Their screams were frightening as they fell into the water. Holt looked around the mass chaos then pushed through the crowd to the bow, which contained fewer people and was practically underwater. Smoke was billowing from the sunken end and got thicker as they approached.

"The lifeboats are the other way," Alex protested, although she wasn't sure if he heard her in all the commotion.

"Those people are already dead; they just don't know it yet," Holt shouted without looking back at her and remained focused on his mission as he pulled her along deck. "They're going to claw at one another until they drown themselves."

Holt stopped by a wooden bench built into the wall, which was partially underwater. From their position, the water collected around their ankles. The massive ship was still visible beneath the water before them. It was a frightening sight. Alex could feel panic flooding her body, but she tried to remain calm.

Holt removed an orange bundle and a life preserver from the bench seat. He tucked the bundle under his arm then roughly shoved her into the life preserver. She thought he'd suffocate her while tightening it. She saw a small mob of people hurrying toward them. Holt cast a look at the crowd coming their way, but it didn't disrupt his focus while attaching her preserver.

"Why are they coming this way?" Alex practically gasped feeling slightly alarmed by the other passengers' fast and furious approach toward them.

"Because they know what I'm holding," he informed her.

Holt removed the bundle from under his arm and pulled the metal ring. The orange bundle flew open and into a small life raft that could only hold four people. He grabbed Alex by the straps on her life preserver and tossed her backward into the raft. She screamed as she flew backward and landed in the raft with a bounce. The massive waves quickly hurled the raft toward the side of the bow still above water.

Alex looked at Holt through the thick smoke. He was swallowed by a group of men attempting to get past him to the raft. The waves violently tossed the raft away from the sinking ship. Alex gasped with horror as she was pulled deeper into the ocean. She felt helpless since all she could do was watch the crowd of men engulfed in the cloud of smoke where Holt once stood.

"Holt!"

As the raft was hurled away, she could see the massive ship was partially submerged in the water. The eerie remanence could still be seen just below the surface. Several people in life preservers jumped overboard and fought the waves to swim for her raft. Their orange life preservers were all she saw as they climbed on top of one another in an attempt to reach her raft.

They just about drown one another while making little headway toward her. She thought about the people onboard, she thought about those possibly drowning in the water, she thought about Holt swallowed by an angry mob, and she thought about her Aunt Trisha. She feared for those who were about to die, but she also feared her uncertain fate. She had no clue what she was supposed to do.

Although she didn't want to die on the ship, she also didn't want to survive all alone. As she watched the orange vests bobbing around the water while men splashed frantically unable to get anywhere, a hand suddenly appeared on the side of the raft. Holt surfaced, heaved himself into the raft, and looked at the men attempting to swim for them. She couldn't describe the relief she'd felt that Holt was alive, although it almost seemed impossible that he'd made it when so many others didn't.

"We should help them," Alex cried out, unable to deal with the relentless screams of those onboard much less those frantically attempting to reach their little raft.

"They'll never make it, and if we went back for them, they'd sink us. There are too many of them," he bluntly informed her.

Alex wasn't sure how she felt about that decision, but she couldn't seem to argue his point. They saw one man swimming for the raft without the signature life preserver. Holt pulled him out of the water and into the raft. Alex was stunned to see it was Bronson. She returned her attention back to the orange life preservers containing people as they were swept into the ocean by the fierce waves. As Bronson gasped to catch his breath, Holt stared at him and shook his head.

"I'm surprised you made it," Holt remarked.

"You can't swim in rough surf wearing a life preserver," Bronson gasped. "That's why the others didn't make it."

"Yes, with waves like this, you have to swim underwater," Holt replied.

Alex finally tore her eyes away from the gruesome sight and stared at Bronson. "Did you see Aunt Trish?" she asked, hoping he'd seen her in one of the lifeboats.

Bronson stared back at her a moment as if at a loss for words then shook his head. "No, but it's possible she made it to one of the lifeboats."

Holt removed two small paddles and handed one to Bronson. "Ever been white water rafting?" he asked while raising a curious brow. "We need to stay on top of the waves or we'll capsize. When the ship goes under, and she will go under, we don't want her taking us with her."

As the two men fought to keep the raft afloat, Alex watched the ship slowly sink. She listened to the horrific screams of the drowning men and women. She could see some crew still attempting to fill lifeboats but most overturned as soon as they reached the water. The waves were too rough, and the large lifeboats couldn't maneuver the waves. She watched with horror as nearly every lifeboat overturned in the rough surf. The passenger's screams lingered.

Before their little raft was even out of sight, she witnessed the ship sink beneath the surface taking every last person with it. As she looked around, she didn't see the lights from any of the lifeboats. Did they all capsize? Bronson and Holt paddled their inflatable raft over the waves, attempting to keep on top of them. Alex clutched her stomach and closed her eyes as the storm continued to beat them from above and below. She didn't mind the pouring rain. At least neither man could see she was crying.

Chapter Seven

It was early morning, and the sun had just come up. The sounds of the ocean and water gently lapping against the side of the raft was almost deafening. Alex lay against Holt, who held her while he slept. She woke nearly twenty minutes earlier but remained nestled against Holt for the warmth. She then felt a hand caress her buttocks. Alex suddenly jumped with alarm and startled Holt. As she turned her head, Bronson jumped away from her and looked around as if disoriented.

"What? What happened?" Bronson cried out.

Alex glared at him, almost certain it hadn't been an accident, but she couldn't be positive. She managed to relax despite her pounding heart. Holt partially sat up after being torn from sleep. He held his head and groaned from his hangover. Alex was about to say something to him when her eyes stared past him.

"Is that--?" she gasped as her eyes lit up. "I see land!"

Holt and Bronson looked in the direction she stared. Despite the thick fog over the ocean, all three could see the outline of a beach in the near distance. Hangover aside, Holt tossed Bronson a paddle and both men paddled through the gentle ocean current toward the only sign of land.

§

The small bonfire burned on the white, sandy beach while the three castaways attempted to warm their damp bodies. The men hung their jackets from bamboo sticks protruding from the ground to help them dry. Holt and Bronson had been soaked from their impromptu swim in the ocean. Alex was thankful her dress was a thin enough material that it dried faster than the men's suits. The fog had finally lifted, allowing Alex to see the beauty of the tropical beach that seemed to extend forever. The edge of the thick woods was fifty yards from the ocean surf. Not much else could be seen beyond the tall trees. The only way to figure out where they were would be to explore their surroundings. Once mostly dry, Holt stood and looked around while sighing.

"We need to find water or this is going to be a short celebration," Holt informed his beach mates.

Bronson frowned and uncertainly ran his fingers through his mostly dry hair. "I've never been camping in my life," he announced. "Are we foolish to believe there will be a rescue anytime soon?"

"We can't wait to find out," Holt replied. "Alex can collect firewood on the beach and keep watch for rescue planes." He then cast a look at Bronson. "We'll look for food and water."

"We don't know what's on this island," Bronson protested. "I'm uncomfortable leaving Alex alone. I should stay with her. She's technically my responsibility."

Holt eyed Bronson and appeared distrusting.

Alex sprang to her feet and joined Holt. "I'll go with Holt to find food and water," she informed Bronson. "You can collect firewood and watch for rescue planes."

Holt gave Alex a strange look. She practically pushed Holt along before anyone could protest. She seemed to be in a hurry until they entered the woods and the beach was out of sight. Holt cast several looks at her.

"What's with you and Bronson?" he finally asked.

"He's lazy, and we're going to carry him if we're stuck here," she informed him then shook her head in disgust. "I don't know what my aunt sees in him. He gives me the creeps."

Holt eyed her, raised a clever brow, and hid his grin. "Something tells me you don't care much for him," he teased.

They exchanged looks and smiled. Her mood immediately changed to concern as she stopped him on the path.

"Seriously, what are we going to do?"

"Well," he announced. "First we're going to look for food and water." He then indicated for her to keep moving.

"He's going to bully us," she sulked without looking at Holt. "I'm just a girl, and you look like a substitute science teacher."

He eyed her suspiciously. "Is that code for nerd?"

Alex grimaced and offered a sympathetic smile. "A cute one--"

He returned his attention to the trail they hiked. "I'll admit, I'm not exactly imposing at 5'9--"

Alex eyed him and sharply raised her brow.

He frowned. "Okay, 5'8"." He gently cleared his throat. "But having been bullied as a boy, I've learned how to deal with people like Bronson." Holt then glared demandingly at her. "And for future reference, I don't want you to ever refer to yourself as 'just a girl'. It's demoralizing to all women."

Alex hid her smile.

Chapter Eight

The sun had already set to a clear evening giving the beach a slight chill off the ocean. The small bonfire was just about ready to go out. Alex sat a few feet from Bronson and shivered in her thin, dress. She always hated dresses, and now that she'd been stuck in this one for over twenty-four hours, she hated dresses even more. Holt returned to the campfire with an armful of wood and dropped it on the sand near Bronson. Holt was clearly irritated.

Bronson glanced from the wood to Holt with a dumbfounded look. "Where did you find the wood?"

"Ironically, in the woods," Holt scoffed.

Holt tossed wood onto the fire while Alex shivered, holding her knees against her chest. Holt removed his jacket and placed it over Alex's shoulders without taking his eyes off Bronson.

"Make no mistake, Bronson," Holt boldly announced while straightening. "Until we're rescued, you will pull your weight around here."

Bronson stared at him with surprise. "Hey, I watched for rescue ships and planes." He then turned defensive. "I can't be in the woods and on the beach at the same time." His eyes suddenly narrowed. "And who put you in charge?"

"As the only person here who's been camping, I put myself in charge," Holt casually informed him.

Bronson glared at him and sneered. "Well, Alex and I don't take orders from you."

Alex clung to Holt's jacket over her shoulders and didn't look away from the fire. "Holt's in charge," she muttered.

Bronson glared at her with disapproval. "You're a minor, and I'm responsible for you."

"It's settled then," Holt announced while straightening proudly as he flopped onto the sand alongside Alex. "I'm in charge." He cast a look at Alex. "And as my first official act, I declare fifteen the age of majority. Alex is responsible for herself."

Alex cast a look at Holt and grinned.

§

Day five. It had been five days since they'd been stranded on the island without so much as seeing another soul from the sunken ship. There hadn't been any planes passing overhead or any ships conveniently sailing past. If there had been a rescue, they weren't looking anywhere near the small island. Alex, Holt, and Bronson walked through the woods while following a small animal trail. There seemed to be trails everywhere. Although the trails were worn, they hadn't run into anything larger than a snake. Holt had pointed it out. Alex was grateful she hadn't seen it. She didn't have much experience with snakes, but she was almost certain they'd be pretty big in the jungle terrain. Bronson lagged behind as usual and appeared bored. Holt walked alongside Alex and pointed at the different types of plant life, telling Alex about each one in great detail.

Alex stared at him with a strange look. "Oh, God," she gasped. "You *are* a science teacher!"

"Not quite," he announced and held back his laugh. "I'm an archeologist."

"Like Indiana Jones?"

"Yeah, but without the bullwhip and fedora," Holt teased.

Despite their night of horror and their desperate situation, Holt rose to the occasion as if he'd spent his entire life training for life as a castaway. Alex would have been concerned, considering it had been five days and they hadn't seen any sign of a rescue, but Holt held it together for her. If she had to be stranded on a deserted island, Holt was her ideal travel companion. Bronson, on the other hand, had gone from annoying to impossible in the last five days.

Bronson groaned, breaking the peacefulness of the jungle, and ran his fingers through his hair. "Does anyone actually know where we are?"

"Yes, Bronson, we're in the woods," Holt casually replied.

"How big is the island?" Alex asked while looking around.

"By my calculations, pretty damned big," Holt informed her then stopped. "Oh, look, mangoes."

All three looked up the tree and admired its height.

Bronson's mouth fell open as he stared up the tree. "A little high up there, Holt."

"I can climb," Alex announced with enthusiasm.

Holt eyed Alex's short, black dress then raised a skeptical brow. "In that?"

"I'll take it off," she replied with little care.

Bronson and Holt stared at her dumbfounded.

"I'd prefer if you didn't," Holt remarked. "And you're looking at some nasty tree burns in some pretty sensitive areas."

"I'm the youngest, and I'm guessing the most flexible," she remarked. "You let me worry about my sensitive areas." Alex indicated the tear in the hem of her dress to Holt. "Rip me."

Holt frowned and ripped the tear on the side of her dress to the top of her thigh. He took a step back and watched as Alex easily scaled the tree. Holt and Bronson stared as Alex moved along the branch containing the mangoes.

"My God," Holt muttered. "She's part monkey."

Alex knocked the mangoes from the branch and smiled at the men on the ground. "Eight years of gymnastics," she proudly announced then started her descent. "I could show you an amazing backward dismount, but I've never done it in a dress."

"I suggest we don't try it either," Holt informed her.

Alex was almost to the bottom when she saw a snake near her. It was quite possibly a boa constrictor, but she didn't actually take time to look at it. She was too busy screaming then tumbled from the tree. Holt and Bronson hurried toward her where she landed. She groaned softly then suddenly screamed and leaped to her feet while looking around.

"Snake! Snake!"

Holt chuckled and pointed up the tree. "Apparently, you scare more easily than the snake."

Alex was momentarily relieved then suddenly gasped and clutched her leg. There was a large cut on her outer thigh, which bled freely. Both men jumped with surprise at the sight of the blood. Holt removed his handkerchief and held it to her injured thigh.

"Is she okay?" Bronson gasped.

Holt peeked at the wound then reapplied pressure to it. "It's not too deep, but we're going to need to clean it and keep it covered. We'll take her back to that stream and soak it."

Chapter Nine

Alex sat on a rock within the stream and cleaned the two-inch cut with Holt's expensive handkerchief, which was now stained pink from the blood. Her injury wasn't too deep, but the sight of the gaping wound turned her stomach. Bronson pulled Holt away from Alex and toward the bank.

"That cut looks pretty bad," Bronson remarked in a hushed tone. "Are you sure she's going to be okay? What are we going to do?"

"We just need to keep it from getting infected," Holt informed him.

"What if it gets infected?"

"Stop worrying. I'll take care of her injury," Holt informed him. "Why don't you go back and collect our lunch before something else does."

Bronson nodded then turned and suddenly stopped. He had a strange look on his face as he stared obviously distracted by what he saw.

"Holt--?"

"What now?" Holt snarled and turned.

They saw a surprisingly clean-shaven man in his late twenties wearing well-preserved clothing with a backpack over his shoulder and a machete in his hand. His dark, nearly black hair was cut businessman short and gave the impression of someone who'd just recently been stranded on the island. His moderately dark tan indicated he'd spent much time outdoors, and his lean build revealed just enough muscle mass to be considered a force in which to be reckoned. The stranger stood on the path near them, staring at them with little expression.

"Who are you?" Damon asked in a low, firm tone meant to intimidate them, which it did.

"We were shipwrecked five days ago," Holt informed him and offered a polite smile. "We're glad to see you. Is there a way off the island?"

"None that I've found," Damon remarked and tilted his head with a curious look. "How many survivors?"

"Just the three of us," Holt replied. "I'm Holt, this is Bronson, and that's Alex over there."

Damon looked past them at Alex in the stream where she sat on the rock in her slightly torn, black dress. He stared at her longer than he should have then looked back at Holt.

"I've been tracking blood," Damon announced and nodded to Alex. "Has she been injured?"

"She cut her leg," Holt replied without taking his eyes off Damon. "Nothing serious."

"Injuries can easily become infected out here," Damon informed him and again eyed Alex.

Alex limped toward them while clutching the handkerchief to her injured thigh. She smiled with embarrassment at possibly the most handsome man she'd ever seen.

"In my defense," she announced teasingly, "it was a really big snake."

Damon continued to stare at her although his expression didn't change. "Yeah, I saw it," he casually replied. "It was a two-footer at best. I assure you, they get a lot bigger than that."

Holt noted the look on Damon's face while he stared at Alex. He stared at her almost as if he had never seen a woman before. Holt immediately tensed, obviously concerned.

Damon looked back at Holt. "Forgive me for being blunt, but my people are very territorial and don't welcome outsiders," he announced. "I can take care of her injury for you, but you'll need to return to the north side of the island."

"Excuse me?" Holt blurted out and stared back at the strange man.

"Not blunt enough? Okay," Damon announced and raised a dark, cocky brow. "My people would assume kill you than share this island with outsiders. Consider that a warning shot across your bow."

All three stared at Damon with surprise.

"Blunt enough for you?" Damon snapped.

"I hear you, but I don't understand the hostility," Holt announced.

"Yeah, well, life sucks," Damon replied while shrugging. "Welcome to my world." He shifted his attention to Alex. "Let's have a look."

Alex took a step toward him. Holt held his hand up, stopping her, but didn't take his eyes off Damon.

"Actually, I'd rather you stayed away from her," Holt announced with little expression.

Damon stared at Holt. Neither man flinched. It was a tense moment. Alex wasn't sure what Holt was doing, but it wasn't wise to piss off the larger, younger man with a machete.

"I don't make house calls," Damon informed him. "If the wound gets infected, she dies."

Alex felt fear flooding her body. She wasn't sure what had Holt suddenly bent out of shape, but she needed to break up the pissing match before it started. Her attention shifted to Holt.

"Holt, please," she announced gently. "It's okay."

Holt maintained his distrusting glare then reluctantly stood aside. Alex sat on a nearby rock and removed the handkerchief from her leg. Damon stared at her a moment then crouched in front of her. He jammed his machete into the ground, startling her. He then removed a first aid kit from his pack and cleaned the wound as if he'd been doing it all his life. Alex cringed, feeling the wound burn from the cleanser.

He eyed her sharply then returned his attention to her injury. "If you think that hurts, you're in for a shock," he remarked.

"Why?" Alex asked with concern.

Damon lifted his eyes and met her gaze for the first time. "I need to stitch it." He then removed a syringe and a bottle from the kit.

Holt saw the syringe and practically bolted for them. Bronson sheepishly stepped into his path while holding up a hand to calm him. The machete had been enough to unnerve Bronson.

"What's that?" Alex asked while staring at the needle with wide, horror-filled eyes. She'd never been a fan of needles, and she could sense something bad was about to happen.

"Sedation and a mild painkiller," he replied simply. He placed his hand on her thigh and applied pressure to keep her leg still. "Okay, say ouch."

"What--?"

Damon stuck the needle in her thigh. Alex yelped with surprise. While the painkiller and sedation cocktail took effect, Holt paced and kept close watch on the strange man. Damon removed a curved needle specifically made for suturing injuries and stitched Alex's leg wound. Whatever he had given her made her feel a little too good. She rested her head against the tree with her eyes closed and giggled as he stitched her wound.

"That tickles."

Damon briefly cast a glance at her between stitches. "Someone's feeling good."

Once he was finished applying six stitches, Damon taped a bandage over the closed wound. Alex watched him as he worked with an unusual seriousness. She admired the handsome man and smiled.

"You're cute."

Holt stopped pacing and stared at the giddy teenager now flirting with the strange and possibly demented man. Damon met her gaze and showed no reaction to the comment, although there was a strange look in his eyes. He packed up his bag, straightened, and handed Holt fresh pads and tape.

"Keep the wound clean and dry," Damon informed him in a gruff tone. "Change the dressing every two days. She should stay off her leg for a few days."

Damon tossed his bag over his shoulder, reclaimed his machete, and headed back for the path. Holt appeared annoyed and hurried after him. Bronson watched with concern. Holt spoke to Damon, although their conversation couldn't be heard. Damon appeared serious and made a motion to Alex while talking. Holt seemed unusually tense. Damon smirked, said something, and walked away. Holt stared after him then finally approached Bronson and Alex. Alex still appeared doped and cheerful.

"What did he say?" Bronson practically gasped.

"What he said isn't important," Holt replied, although he was clearly upset by what he'd heard. "We need to leave them alone at all costs. We're never to go beyond this stream again. We'll stay on the north side of the island."

"He said something that got to you, didn't he?" Bronson announced with alarm in his eyes. "What did he say?"

"It's not important. He and his people are hostile, and that's all we need to know," Holt informed him then gestured wildly with his hands. "Let's get Alex back to our beach. The sooner we're away from here, the better I'll feel."

"What about the mangoes?"

"Forget the mangoes!"

Holt helped Alex to her feet with a little, added vigor, surprising her with his strength. She leaned on his shoulder and smiled with giddy delight.

"Dr. Jones, I presume," she giggled.

Holt forced a smile at her mildly giddy state. "Yes."

Chapter Ten

Day seven. It was another beautiful morning in paradise despite that Alex wasn't particularly in the mood to enjoy it. Alex sat on the beach, grateful for the warm sun warding off her chill from the previous night. She gingerly rubbed her injured leg while staring out at the horizon over the ocean at the vast nothingness. She saw Bronson approach from the surf while carrying a soaked, orange life preserver. He tossed it to the sand and collapsed alongside her. She briefly glanced at him but didn't want to pay too much attention to him.

"I guess the tide is starting to wash up debris from the wreckage," Bronson informed her.

She finally cast a look at him and appeared concerned. "No chance anyone else survived?" she asked. "Maybe Aunt Trish--?"

Bronson shook his head while frowning. Alex felt a surge of pain sweep through her thigh. She cringed and rubbed her leg.

"Are you okay?" he asked.

"Yeah, just sore from sitting around for two days," she replied and again cringed as her leg ached. "My thigh is cramping."

"Let me help." Bronson placed his hand beneath Alex's thigh and massaged it with some force.

Alex gasped from the fierceness of his gripping hand and cringed. Despite the pain he seemed to cause, it actually made it feel a little better.

"Yeah, that's where it hurts."

As Bronson worked out the cramp on the back of her thigh, his hand slid further up her leg in a more caressing manner. Alex tensed and stopped him while simultaneously pulling back her leg.

"It's better, thanks."

Bronson smiled and straightened. Alex cast a look at him and remained tense. She looked around the beach, wishing Holt would return soon. She didn't like being alone with Bronson longer than necessary.

"Holt's been gone a while," she remarked. "Maybe we should look for him."

"He's fine," Bronson assured her. "One week and he can already find his way around the woods with his eyes closed."

"I wish I could be out there exploring the island too," she pouted.

"Considering your last outing, you're probably better off remaining here on the beach," Bronson informed her while indicating her injury.

Alex frowned and sank into her own world. Anything was better than talking with Bronson. She didn't care for him as her aunt's boyfriend, and she liked him less now that she was stranded on an island with him. Holt bolted from the woods, startling them. He hurried toward them and pulled Alex to her feet. She would have been concerned, but his boyish smile told them he found something of interest.

"You won't believe what I've found," he announced excitedly. "It's about a twenty-minute walk from here, but it's worth it."

Chapter Eleven

Alex was having a difficult time keeping up with Holt, who clung to her hand while practically dragging her along the path. He wouldn't allow her to walk any further than their makeshift bathroom for two days, and now he was dragging her through the jungle at a brisk jog. She couldn't deny the muscles in her legs were protesting. The three finally appeared in the clearing and stared at a lighthouse set along the cliff towering majestically above the world. A small caretaker's cabin of sorts was attached to the lighthouse.

The lighthouse soared three stories above the cabin. Although its paint job was faded, there was still some remanence of the red and white candy cane swirl design. The glass panels surrounding the light on top remained intact despite decades of neglect. Apart from needing a good cleaning, the glass was surprisingly free of breaks and cracks. Bronson and Alex were stunned at the discovery, which seemed almost unbelievable. Holt approached the small cabin attached to the lighthouse and looked back at them while grinning.

"Wait until you see the best part," he announced excitedly.

Alex and Bronson followed Holt into the lighthouse living quarters. Despite only being one room, the cabin was larger than it seemed from the outside. There was an old bunk bed attached to the wall, a sturdy, handmade table with benches large enough to seat four, a stone kitchen with fire pit, and a handmade armoire filled with old, musty clothing.

"We have oil for lamps, candles, blankets, clothing, and towels," Holt announced cheerfully. "There's a kitchen for cooking and beds. The stairs lead up to the lighthouse. If the light works, we can watch for passing ships and signal them."

Alex looked around and felt some relief yet a pang of concern. "This is great," she announced while gently rubbing her chilled arms. "I never thought a dark, dirty, dingy room would look so good."

"We'll clean it up and make it livable for now," Holt informed her with enthusiasm. "There are buckets, rags, and cleaning supplies. We should start with the linens, so we have a place to sleep tonight."

"I'm going to check out the lighthouse," Bronson announced with enthusiasm and hurried up the sturdy, old stairs.

Alex approached the handmade bunk bed against the wall and ran her hand along the dusty, plush quilt. The mattresses weren't thick, but the bed beneath was solid wood, which would keep them firm. The top bunk was the size of a twin bed, and the bottom bunk was a full-size bed. Alex pulled back the dusty comforter and drifted out a moment.

Holt curbed his enthusiasm while staring at her. "Is something wrong?" he asked. "I thought you'd be happy with actual shelter."

She snapped out of her trance. "No, this is--" She hesitated and forced an insincere smile. "This is great."

Holt's enthusiasm faded. He approached her, placed his hand on her shoulder, and appeared concerned. "Something *is* wrong."

Alex frowned. "It's nothing," she announced. "It's probably just me."

She pulled the dusty comforter off the bed and let it fall to the dirty floor. Holt forced her to face him and looked into her eyes.

"Rule number one," he announced. "Always trust your instincts, Alex. Rule number two. Always tell me what's bothering you no matter how trivial it seems."

"I thought rule number one was stay away from the south side of the island?" she teased, attempting to lighten the mood.

"That's not a rule, that's a commandment," he corrected. "What's bothering you?"

She fidgeted and ran her fingers through her mussed hair. "I'm just very uncomfortable around Bronson," she replied. "I can't put my finger on a specific reason. I mean, he's been more helpful lately."

"But he still gives you the creeps."

"I just can't help feeling these quarters are too close with Bronson in the picture."

"Don't worry, Alex," he announced. "You get the top bunk to yourself. No one's suggesting you share the bottom bunk with Bronson."

"I'd actually feel better if I slept in the lighthouse," she muttered and insecurely rubbed her arms.

Holt muttered, "I'd feel better if *Bronson* slept in the lighthouse."

Alex managed a tiny laugh, placed her arms around his neck, and hugged him. He held her against him and returned the embrace. Bronson appeared on the stairs, causing Holt to release Alex.

"I think the light will work," Bronson announced. "There's plenty of kerosene, and I saw some fresh wicks in a crate up there."

Holt straightened proudly while studying Bronson as he reached the bottom of the steps. "How would you feel about bunking in the crow's nest?"

"Awesome view, but I think I should stay down here with Alex," Bronson replied then offered a strange smile. "You can have the crow's nest."

Holt's look hardened and turned serious. "I think it would be best if you slept upstairs."

Bronson and Holt stared at each other in some bizarre sort of standoff.

"Could I have a word with you outside?" Bronson finally asked and nodded toward the door.

"Of course."

Bronson and Holt stepped outside and partially closed the door behind them. Alex peered out the opening and attempted to eavesdrop on their conversation.

"I don't know what you're up to, but I'm uncomfortable with the way you've been acting around Alex," Bronson announced while glaring at Holt.

Holt stared at the younger man with a stunned look. "Excuse me?"

"Save the charm for the kids on the playground," Bronson snarled. "You're trying to turn Alex against me so you can bang her."

Holt stiffened while glaring into Bronson's eyes. "Okay, all politeness aside." His look turned cold and hateful. "I don't like you. You have no respect for women and even less respect for me because you think I'm weak." His eyes then narrowed. "I've been trying to overlook your character flaws, but if you ever again imply my intentions toward Alex are anything but honorable, I'm going to put you in the ground."

His words were moderately startling. Alex held back her gasp and suddenly feared for Holt's welfare. Bronson didn't have much of a temper, but he wasn't one to back down from a fight, particularly when his opponent was smaller and older.

"Don't threaten me," Bronson growled while sneering at the man he towered over. "You're quickly outliving your usefulness. Alex is my responsibility not yours, and I want you to stay away from her."

Holt's eyes suddenly narrowed. "I believe this is the part where I say 'make me'."

Without hesitation, Bronson swung at Holt. Alex gasped with horror and threw open the door just in time to see Holt block the punch. He caught Bronson's arm, twisted it behind his back, and drove him to his knees. Bronson cried out unable to move. Holt glared at the immobile man now screaming in agony.

"Make no mistake, I could easily dislocate your shoulder or break your arm, but I'm afraid we might need you," Holt snarled at him in a tone that surprised Alex. "Keep that in mind the next time you challenge me, because I won't hold back if you piss me off again."

Holt released his wrist and allowed him to fall forward. When Holt looked at the doorway, he saw Alex staring at him with surprise. Holt frowned and fidgeted slightly.

"I'm sorry you had to see that."

Chapter Twelve

Five months later. It was early afternoon and another beautiful, sunny day in paradise. Holt was on the small beach located down the path from the lighthouse. The beach was isolated from the rest of the island beaches, and Holt was often found there in the early afternoon. The bluffs on either side kept the beach secluded. In his bare feet, he practiced karate moves in slow motion as if performing yoga. Alex ran onto the beach with a sense of urgency. Despite being in a hurry, Alex stopped to watch and held back her laugh.

"So you're a karate, ass-kicking archeologist?" she teased.

Holt turned with surprise and appeared embarrassed. "I thought you were mango hunting."

"Why didn't you tell me you knew karate?" she asked while grinning.

"Because you'd want to learn," he replied.

"Hell, yeah!"

"I taught you how to defend yourself," he informed her then resumed his practice. "Karate should only be taught by those qualified to teach it."

"Oh, please," she whined. "We're stuck here until the end of time. Who's going to know?"

"I made that mistake once."

Alex stared at him with surprise and immediately wondered what he was keeping from her. "Why? What happened?"

"I don't want to talk about it."

She frowned her disapproval. "I wish you'd remember that phrase when you're rambling on about foliage," she muttered.

Holt chuckled and cast a look at her. "What's the urge in urgency?"

Her grin soon returned, and her eyes lit up. "I found something," she announced excitedly. "I didn't touch it, but you have to come see it."

Holt didn't bother questioning her finding and was willing to entertain her whims, but that didn't mean he was ever in a hurry. He casually slipped into his shoes in no particular rush. Alex groaned, grabbed his hand, and pulled him toward the woods before he even had his foot in his shoe. Holt hurried behind Alex, who dragged him by the hand.

"I swear, Alex, if you're dragging me out here to kill another spider--"

"No, it's not a spider," she exclaimed with excitement. "It's an *it.*"

"An it?"

"As in 'not yet identified'."

"Really?" he gasped with surprise then pushed her. "Move, girl!"

Holt ran along the path behind Alex. They slowed near a long, flowing crystal clear stream close to the south side of the island. Alex crouched near a rock. Holt moved alongside her. There was a small, black creature about the size of a football with a tail nearly as long resting between two rocks within the stream. The creature had a smooth, tough exterior rather than skin or fur, indicating it was possibly reptilian in nature. The small creature wailed softly as if in pain.

Holt stared at it with a look of surprise. "What the hell is that?"

She looked at him as her eyes widened. "You mean you don't know either?"

"I have no clue," Holt replied then gently touched the creature with a stick.

Alex folded her arms across her chest and glared at him. "I could have poked it with a stick."

"I think it's hurt," he announced. "Go back to the house, grab that small crate, line it with cloth, and get those heavy gloves by the fire pit."

§

The one-room cabin off the lighthouse was clean and homey, having come a long way since they first discovered the building five months earlier. Light brightened the cabin through the open, glassless windows with old-fashioned, wooden shutters to keep out the elements. Alex, Holt, and Bronson kneeled around the cloth-filled crate containing the small, black creature. The unusual creature cried and attempted to stand up in the soft bedding. It fell down several times.

"I think its leg is hurt," Holt remarked.

Alex stared at him with concern for the creature's life. "You think it's broken?"

"There's only one way to find out," Holt replied with a tense sigh.

Holt stuck his hand into the crate and touched the creature's leg. The creature scratched and bit him despite having no teeth and dull claws. Holt flinched with surprise by the aggressive attack but continued to feel the creature's back leg.

"I don't think it's broken," Holt announced then sat back on his feet and appeared to weigh his options. "Let's just give it some time to heal. Our little friend will need some food and water." He looked back at Alex. "See if you can find something small to use for a water dish. I'll see if it likes mango."

"What is it?" Bronson finally asked.

"Nothing I've ever seen," Holt admitted. "I'm pretty sure it's just a baby though. It didn't have any teeth-- thankfully."

Alex put a small bowl of water into the crate. The creature drank for several minutes.

Alex gave Holt a sly look and grinned. "Can we keep it?" she asked.

Holt groaned and rolled his eyes as if anticipating the question. "We don't even know what it is yet, Alex," he remarked.

Alex watched as Holt placed some sliced mango into the crate. The creature sniffed the mango, picked it up with its front paws, and ate it.

"Well, it likes fruit," Holt deducted. "Reassuring in case we run into mom."

"Why haven't we seen anything like this the last five months?" Bronson asked. "It's obviously a baby. Shouldn't we have seen the mother?"

"That is puzzling," Holt replied. "I doubt this little guy is much older than three months. You'd think we'd have run into the mother at some point."

The creature sneezed.

"Oh, that's so adorable," Alex cooed.

Bronson shook his head while frowning.   "Only girls would find snot adorable."

Chapter Thirteen

That night, Holt slept peacefully in the lower bunk while Alex slept in the upper bunk above him. The room was dimly lit by a small fire burning in the kitchen fire pit. The creature wailed softly from the crate. Alex woke, jumped from the top bunk, and sat on the floor by the crate. The creature now stood on its hind legs. It had its front paws on the top of the crate and looked over the edge at her.

"Do you miss your mommy?" Alex asked while studying the creature. "Me too."

Alex placed her hand close to the creature's face. It sniffed her hand but showed no aggression. She gently stroked its head and body. It cooed softly. The sound was pleasing, indicating it was possibly friendly. Alex picked it up and held it against her chest. The creature nuzzled her and continued to coo, almost like a cat purring.

"It's okay," she announced while rocking the creature. "I'll look after you."

Holt lay on his bunk and watched Alex while she mothered the orphaned creature. He smiled and shut his eyes.

§

The following day, Holt looked around the stream where they had found the creature. Alex sat on a large rock and studied him while he studied the area. She spent a lot of time watching Holt while he studied things that bored her.

"You're so serious when you're in archeologist mode," she commented.

"Where does this stream originate?"

"I don't know," she replied with humor. "Beyond my boundaries." Her eyes suddenly lit up. "Want me to find out?"

"No," Holt firmly replied without looking at her while continuing to study the area. "I think our little guy was washed downstream. Maybe from that storm we had last week. Nothing indicates he lived in this area. Maybe that's why we've never seen its mother."

Alex cocked her head and grimaced. "Are you looking for Monster poop?"

"Seriously?" Holt announced and finally looked at her. "Is that what you're calling him?"

She shrugged then grinned. "It's fitting. He's a little monster."

Holt appeared distracted, frowned, and looked upstream.

Alex hid her grin while watching him. She could just about see his mind working.

"You want to go upstream, don't you?" she remarked. "You have that look on your face."

He glanced at her and cocked his head. "And what look is that, my dear?"

"That 'let's break the peace treaty in the name of science' look," she teased.

"I'm a bad influence on you."

"Don't be too hard on yourself," she replied casually. "I'm entering the rebellious stage. I'm my own bad influence."

Holt suddenly chuckled and smiled at her. "Oh, that's right," he announced cheerfully. "You have a birthday coming up, don't you?"

"I couldn't tell you," she replied. "I don't even know what month it is."

"It's October 13th."

She stared at him with some surprise. "Really? How do you know that?"

"I'm a genius with an eidetic memory, remember?" he reminded her then grinned. "Three days, huh? The big one-six. I suppose you're going to want the keys to my car."

"Depends," she announced with interest. "What do you drive?"

"A Bentley."

She frowned in response. "Sounds boring."

"My wife has a Ferrari."

Alex suddenly perked up and beamed with delight. "Sold."

He laughed in response. "If we get back before all of my assets are auctioned off, you can have the Ferrari," he announced.

"Cool."

He gave her a serious look. "Don't forget to feed your little monster."

Alex jumped up, happy for the reminder. "Oh, yeah. I almost forgot," she announced and was about to leave. She paused, turned back toward him, and kissed him quickly on the cheek while grinning. "Thanks for the car."

Chapter Fourteen

Alex sat on the cabin floor with the little creature on her lap while feeding it mango slices. It held the fruit between its front paws and ate like a squirrel. Bronson appeared at the bottom of the stairs, having come down from the lighthouse.

"I thought I heard someone," he announced then approached. "Weren't you off exploring with the professor?"

"I needed to feed Monster," she replied without looking at him and kept her attention on her strange new pet.

Bronson shook his head and sat on the floor near her where she held the creature.

"Are you seriously keeping that thing?"

"Holt said I could," she replied.

"And if he said you couldn't?"

"I suppose I'd have to defy him, but it's expected," she casually replied. "I'm rebelling."

"You? Rebelling?" he asked while snorting a laugh. "Sorry, I hadn't noticed."

"Well, according to the calendar, I'm turning sixteen in three days."

"What calendar?" he practically demanded and glanced around the cabin.

"The calendar in Holt's head."

"Sixteen, huh?" Bronson remarked then chuckled. "That's an important birthday." He then considered. "Although not so much without access to a car. Maybe we could find another way to celebrate your sweet sixteen."

She looked at him with an enthusiastic look in her eyes. "Cliff diving?"

"Hmm, I don't think so. Did you see the bottom of that cliff? You'd break your neck on those rocks," he remarked.

"There's water at the bottom of the one not far from the mango trees," she informed him.

"Nice try," he remarked. "No cliff diving." Bronson then sank into thought. "I feel bad; we can't even bake you a cake."

"It's okay. I have a new pet," she replied. "Monster can be my birthday gift."

Alex held the creature in her arms like a baby. Bronson touched the creature, allowing his arm to brush past her chest. Alex tensed, realized it must have been an innocent accident, and attempted to ignore it.

The following morning, Holt was on the beach practicing his karate in slow motion. Alex walked onto the beach, paused when she saw him, and attempted to imitate his movements.

Holt looked back and chuckled. "Stop that. You're breaking my concentration."

"I know what you can give me for my birthday," she announced enthusiastically.

He didn't allow her to interfere with his practice. "No, I'm not teaching you karate."

Alex frowned while sitting on a nearby rock. She watched Holt practice a moment longer then stared off and appeared distant. "Holt--?"

"Alex."

She drew a deep breath and held it. "I've been feeling very uncomfortable around Bronson lately," she gently informed him.

"Really?" he replied while continuing with his routine. "I've found him almost tolerable. He seems to treat you with more respect since I nearly broke his arm."

"It just seems like--" She hesitated then frowned. "I don't know."

"Rule number two," he announced firmly without looking back at her.

"It seems like every time you're not around, he does things that make me uncomfortable," she finally blurted out her concerns then groaned.

Holt suddenly stopped and turned toward her with an odd look. "Give me a 'for instance'."

She ran her fingers through her hair. "I'm probably just being stupid."

Holt approached and sat on the rock alongside her. "Let me decide that."

"There's something about the way he smiles at me, and I swear he's always looking down my shirt," she announced then hesitated. "Then there's the way he touches me--"

Holt's expression suddenly hardened. "What way does he touch you?"

Chapter Fifteen

Later that evening, Holt and Bronson walked through the woods along their usual path toward the area containing coconut trees. Everything they needed to survive comfortably was only a five to fifteen-minute walk from the lighthouse. Holt seemed distracted for the first few minutes then finally perked up.

"I'm glad you suggested planning something special for Alex's birthday," Holt announced as they walked. "I had a few thoughts of my own."

"I thought if we could get a few coconuts, we could grind up the coconut meat with the milk, add a little of that sugarcane, and come up with something fudge-like," Bronson replied and managed a sly grin.

Holt again drifted out a moment. He drew a deep breath and cast a look at Bronson. He could no longer hold back his emotions. "Now that we're alone, we need to discuss something that's been bothering me."

Bronson eyed Holt as they approached a coconut tree not far from the bluffs then pointed up the tree.

"I'm a poor climber," Bronson announced as if avoiding the conversation.

"Seriously, we need to discuss Alex," Holt pressed with limited patience.

"Can we discuss Alex while you're knocking down coconuts?" Bronson questioned.

"No, we can't."

Bronson frowned and indicated for Holt to continue, although he appeared bored already.

"You've been making unwanted advances," Holt boldly informed him.

Bronson stared at him with surprise. "Advances? What advances? You have your hands on her more than I do," he protested then attempted to relax. "I'm not trying to pick a fight or accuse you of anything." He managed a nervous laugh. "Don't break my arm."

"She doesn't want you touching her, and I intend to enforce her wishes," Holt announced.

"We seem to have a little problem, Holt," Bronson announced while folding his arms across his chest. "She told me the same thing about you."

"She never told you any such thing."

"She's a teenager," Bronson remarked and sighed. "They tend to make things up, especially when they're trying to control a situation."

"This is about you, Bronson," Holt interjected and pointed a warning finger at him. "Don't try to make it about me."

"She's playing you, Holt, and I can prove it," he announced while glaring at him. "When we get back, we'll confront her on her lies."

"Fine, we'll go back and ask Alex," Holt announced then indicated the path to the lighthouse.

Bronson smirked and pointed at the coconuts. "I didn't come all the way out here for the exercise."

Holt groaned then headed for the tree and looked up it. "I hate being short."

He made his moderately slow attempt at climbing the tree. Bronson removed a thick branch from behind a nearby tree and swung, hitting Holt in the back. Holt fell from the tree and landed roughly. Despite his rough landing, he rolled to his feet to face Bronson. Bronson swung again and struck him in the head. Holt fell to the ground and appeared unconscious. Bronson tossed the branch aside, grabbed Holt by the ankles, and dragged him toward the bluffs. Holt regained consciousness just near the bluffs and attempted to grab Bronson despite his head injury. Bronson kicked Holt in the side several times and sent him over the edge of the bluffs. There was a moment of silence, and a splash followed.

Bronson grinned. "So long, Holt."

Chapter Sixteen

Alex walked along the beach the following morning and looked in Holt's usual area for him. She was worried about him when he didn't come home last night. There was no sign of Holt, and she was growing concerned. Bronson appeared on the beach from the path and jogged to catch up with her.

"You got up early," he called out and stopped near her. Bronson immediately pulled Alex into his arms and kissed her on the cheek. "Happy birthday, Alex."

She felt slightly uncomfortable, but it was just an innocent birthday wish. "Thank you." Alex pulled away and looked around while insecurely rubbing her arms. "I haven't seen Holt since yesterday evening. It's not like him to be gone overnight."

"Oh, I'm not about to spoil his birthday surprise for you," Bronson announced with a low chuckle. "He'll be back later, I promise."

Alex felt relieved by his words and immediately smiled. "He's doing something special for my birthday?" she remarked and attempted to brush off her anxiety. "He's been gone so long. What could he be doing?"

"Probably building you a car out of coconuts," Bronson teased then chuckled at his own joke. "I have a special surprise for you myself, but I need to prepare, so you just go out and do whatever it is you do."

As Bronson returned to the path, Alex could only think of one thing she wanted to do at that moment. She wanted to find Holt even if it meant ruining whatever surprise he had for her. She just needed to know he was okay. Nothing else mattered.

§

By late afternoon, Alex walked along the stream where they had originally found Monster. Despite Bronson's reassurances, she wasn't convinced Holt had spent the entire evening and night doing something special for her birthday. She was concerned he may have attempted to find out more about Monster's origins, which could be hazardous to his health. She looked at the ground near the stream and appeared frustrated.

"Come on, Alex. You've watched him look at the ground and flora for months," she muttered while staring at the ground. "You should be able to track him."

Although it seemed to take some time, she finally found a set of tracks. Alex followed them along the stream, stopped to eye some plants, and then continued onward. Alex paused near a tree and looked at the damp base. She appeared curious then crouched down and dabbed her finger to the moist ground. She smelled the substance then suddenly cringed, sprang to her feet, and wiped her fingers on the tree.

"Oh, God--urine! Gross!"

Alex followed the tracks on the path toward the bluffs. Instead of one set, there were now several sets of tracks. Some appeared fresher than others. Alex approached the clearing containing the coconut trees. She crouched near the tree and saw droplets of blood on the ground and on nearby plants. Alex looked at the thick, oddly placed branch with blood on it.

She then noticed the deep drag marks and more blood on the ground not far from the tree. Alex followed the drag marks nearly fifty yards to the bluffs and suddenly stopped. She saw Damon crouched near the edge of the bluffs alongside the end of the drag marks. Alex took a step back as horror swept through her entire body. Damon glanced back, saw her, and straightened with his machete in his hand. Alex gasped and ran for the path.

Chapter Seventeen

It was nearly dark by the time Alex returned to the lighthouse. She was exhausted from her long day of searching for Holt with no success. She didn't know what had happened to him, but she was entertaining several horrible scenarios already. If something happened to Holt, she didn't know how she'd ever survive on the island without him. As she entered the lighthouse, Bronson stared at her and appeared surprised.

"Where have you been?" he asked. "You've been gone all day."

"Looking for Holt," she announced and couldn't hide her concern. "I think that man killed him."

"What man?"

"The one from the south side of the island," she announced while attempting to fight her tears. "The scary one with the machete!"

Bronson approached her and placed his hands on her shoulders to calm her. He stared at her with concern.

"Tell me what happened."

Alex attempted to relax and caught her breath. "I was tracking Holt, and I found blood. It looked as if someone had been dragged to the bluffs. When I got there, I saw *him*."

"You saw the man from the other side of the island at the bluffs?"

Alex nodded and wiped her tears. "He saw me, and I ran. Holt wasn't there," she explained. "I think he stabbed him and tossed him off the bluffs. I went to the beach, but I didn't find him."

Bronson pulled Alex into his arms and held her. "Oh, that must have been terrifying. You're lucky you got away."

She half-heartedly returned the embrace. "I don't know why he didn't chase me."

Bronson guided her to the bottom bunk and sat alongside her while keeping his arm firmly around her shoulders.

"It's going to be dark soon, but first thing tomorrow morning, we're going to go back to the bluffs and have a look," he insisted. "We'll find Holt, I promise."

Alex sniffed and again wiped her tears. "I think he's dead. I think that man killed him." She shook her head. "It's possible Holt may have gone to the south side of the island looking for evidence of Monster's origin. Maybe that man caught him."

Alex sobbed, feeling it was all her fault. She couldn't live with herself if Holt died because of her.

"It's okay, Alex," he reassured her while holding her against his shoulder. "I'm going to take care of you. I promise."

When she lifted her head, Bronson suddenly kissed her on the lips. Alex gasped with surprise and pushed him back.

"What do you think you're doing?" she gasped in horror.

"I'm taking care of you, Alex. Just as I promised," he replied then attempted to kiss her again.

She attempted to hold him back while glaring at him with hostility. "I don't want you taking care of me that way! Let go of me!"

Bronson tackled her to the bed and maintained his smile while she attempted to push him off her. "Trust me; it's better this way. Holt was in the way," he informed her. "Now it's just the two of us."

Alex stopped struggling and stared at him with a look of horror. "It was you, wasn't it?" she gasped. Her horror turned to rage. "You bastard!"

Alex rammed her forehead into his nose. Bronson clutched his nose allowing her the opportunity to throw him off her. As he toppled to the floor, she ran for the door. Bronson sprang up from the floor and tackled her against the door. She hit the door harshly and gasped as pain shot through her body. He spun her around and pinned her against the door with his body. She was momentarily dazed from the hard hit. Monster stood up in his box and wailed while watching, his little tail thrashing wildly.

Bronson glared into her eyes with an anger she'd never seen before. "You need to learn to respect me if you want me to take care of you."

"I want you to go to hell!"

Bronson backhanded Alex across the face, stunning her. Monster again wailed loudly. Bronson held her shoulders and shook her.

"I'm it, Alex," he lashed out. "I'm all you've got. So you'd better get used to it."

Bronson grabbed her wrists and pulled her toward the bed. Alex fought him and attempted to kick him in the groin. He blocked the kick then shoved her onto the bed, enraged by her attempt to maim him. Her head struck the upper bunk. Alex clutched her head and fell to the lower bunk while momentarily dazed. Monster again wailed while thrashing his tail, rocking the crate. Bronson unbuttoned his pants then grabbed Alex's shorts. She still appeared unable to move or defend herself. Bronson suddenly jumped with surprise. The twelve-inch creature scaled Bronson's pants leg while snarling softly as his foot-long tail swished wildly. Bronson jumped with surprise.

Monster leaped onto his forearm, clung to his shirt with tiny, cat-like claws digging into his skin, and attempted to bite him with his toothless mouth. Bronson screamed and slung his arm violently. Monster flew off his arm and across the bed. Bronson looked at the bed. Monster was gone! Alex felt the room stop spinning long enough to open her eyes and witness Bronson grabbing her shorts. She cried out and kicked at him while attempting to keep him away from her. He fought her hands and thrashing legs for control of her shorts. They heard a tiny, fierce snarl.

Bronson looked up with surprise to the sound. Monster hung by his claws from the upper bunk and leaped upside down for Bronson's face. Bronson cried out as Monster's claws dug into his cheeks while he tried in vain to bite his nose with his toothless mouth. His tail thrashed wildly, thumping Bronson on the top of his head with enough force to cause him to wince. Alex kicked Bronson in the abdomen. He stumbled backward and struck the table while attempting to dislodge Monster from his face. Alex jumped to her feet and staggered dizzily while holding her head. Bronson pulled Monster from his face, revealing deep puncture wounds and long scratches. He threw the thrashing, wailing creature across the floor.

Monster struck the floor, letting out a sharp cry, and rolled several times from the force. He suddenly flipped onto his feet, hissed his anger, and raced up the wall. Alex stumbled toward the door, knowing she had to escape, but she couldn't move fast enough in her disoriented condition. Bronson again grabbed her from behind and tossed her back onto the bed. Alex screamed and fought Bronson, who was now on top of her, using his body to pin her to the bed. He pawed at her shorts like a wild man, attempting to slip them down her hips. Monster scurried under the top bunk and dove onto Bronson's back, digging in with his claws, and letting out a fierce, tiny roar. Bronson attempted to remove the creature without releasing Alex, but he was planted firmly on the center of his back and thrashed his tail, cracking Bronson's hand each time he attempted to grab him.

The front door was thrown open with a thunderous crash, startling everyone. Monster cried out with surprise and leaped off Bronson. Bronson jerked with surprise from his position on top of Alex and looked at the door. Holt stood just inside the doorway, soaking wet, bruised, and scratched. He charged for Bronson. Bronson leaped off Alex and attempted to move out of his path.

"Holt--?" Bronson gasped.

Alex sat up with surprise, clutched her head, and attempted to focus on the soaking wet man. Holt stopped just short of Bronson. Bronson held his hands out and appeared terrified.

"Holt, I'm sorry," Bronson cried out in panic. "It won't happen again!"

Holt stood completely still while staring at Bronson with a cold, psychotic look in his eyes. His eyes strayed to the blood on Alex's hand and the tears down her face as she stared back. Holt suddenly spun into a high roundhouse kick and struck Bronson in the face. He dropped to the floor with a thud. He gingerly touched his bleeding face then looked at Hold and again held up his hands defensively. He slowly moved to his feet.

"Just give me another chance," Bronson begged while straightening.

Holt stared at him through squinting eyes. There was no emotion left; only hatred. Bronson suddenly lunged for Holt, throwing a fist at his face. Holt blocked the punch and kicked him in the hip. As he started to fall, Holt grabbed him around the neck and swiftly snapped it, breaking his neck. He released Bronson, allowing him to drop to the floor. Holt stood over the motionless man and resumed his cold stance. Alex stared in horror at the dead man on the floor. Her heart was pounding in unison with her aching head. Holt exhaled as the emotion returned to his face. He looked back at Alex, practically fell to his knees before her on the bunk, clasped her hands in his, and stared into her eyes.

"Are you okay?"

Alex burst into tears, threw her arms around him, and fell onto her knees with him. They clung to each other and sobbed together in a small huddle. Monster leaped onto her shoulder, clung upside down to her arm around Holt, curled his long tail around them both, and wailed softly with them.

Chapter Eighteen

After Holt changed into dry clothing, he wrapped Bronson's body in a burlap sack and tied it securely with some old rope. Alex subconsciously stroked the purring creature in her arms while she sat on the floor and watched Holt plot his disposal of Bronson's body. She was filled with nervous anxiety over everything that had happened that evening.

"What are we going to do with him?" she asked timidly.

"Burial at sea," he scoffed.

"The bluffs?"

Holt nodded then picked the body up by the ropes near the chest and dragged it toward the door. Alex hurried to join him, took the ropes by the ankles, and helped him move the body. Holt glanced at her and managed a tiny, grateful smile. Alex and Holt pulled the body from the lighthouse and into the partially moonlit night. To Alex's surprise and possible horror, Damon leaned against a tree in the woods and watched them. Alex gasped and nearly dropped Bronson's bound legs.

"Don't worry about him," Holt casually replied without looking at the man.

When she looked back into the woods, Damon was gone. "What did he want?"

"Just making sure I got home."

Alex stared at him with some surprise. "He helped you?"

"In his own macabre, narcissistic way," Holt replied then briefly eyed her. "Make no mistake; that doesn't make him our ally."

Alex again looked at the woods hoping to catch a glimpse of the mysterious man. Is that what he was doing by the bluffs when she saw him? Was he attempting to figure out what happened to Holt as well? She wasn't stupid enough to trust him, but she found it hard not to accept him as their ally if he saved Holt's life. What possible reason would he have to help Holt? There had to be good in the man. As she helped drag Bronson's wrapped corpse to the nearby bluffs, a thousand thoughts raced through her mind.

They took a moment to rest while Holt peered over the ledge to the beach below. Just a few yards further there was nothing but ocean. They toted the body a few yards over and then pushed the bundle over the edge. Alex straightened and watched Bronson's body plummet into the water below. For a moment, she almost felt sorry for him. For some odd reason, her aunt loved the man. Her pity quickly ended when she imagined him tossing Holt off a similar bluff further from the lighthouse, purposely trying to end his life so he could turn her into his personal plaything. She suddenly felt sorry for her Aunt Trisha. At least she didn't live long enough to know what sort of man she'd invited into her life.

§

Nearly an hour later, Holt kneeled before Alex where she insecurely sat on the lower bunk. He gently touched her hands folded on her lap and frowned while eying the bruises on her wrists and face. She wasn't sure if he was sad, sickened, or angry at what Bronson had done to her. Sorrow seemed to win.

"I'm really sorry, Alex," he practically whispered while gently caressing her hands.

She met his gaze with some surprise. "It wasn't your fault. He nearly killed you."

He drew a deep breath and stared into her eyes. "Yes, it is my fault," Holt informed her and again frowned. "I should have seen through him. I should have taken action immediately when you told me your concerns. I should never have turned my back on him." Holt stood while holding her hands, pulled her to her feet, and stared into her eyes. His anger seemed to resurface. "I should have trained you to defend yourself better." He held his breath while keeping his hostility under control. "Starting tomorrow, I'm teaching you everything I know about martial arts so something like this will never happen again."

Alex smiled overjoyed and threw her arms around his neck. "Thank you!"

Holt held her a long moment then finally pulled away. A pleased smile suddenly crossed his face.

"Oh, I almost forgot--" He approached his wet pants on the bench and removed a single pearl attached to a braided cord. He handed her the homemade bracelet. "Happy birthday, dear."

Alex affectionately touched the pearl on the bracelet and grinned with delight while meeting his gaze.

"I love it," she proclaimed. "Thank you!" She again hugged him.

Chapter Nineteen

Six years later. Alex slept peacefully on the top bunk. It was just a little after sunup when she woke to something loud rattling around outside. She jumped gracefully from the bunk, landing softly on the floor in her bare feet. Alex had grown into a beautiful woman and looked even more like her aunt. Her long, dark hair was moderately wild despite daily brushings. Too much time on the beach and roaming the jungle kept her hair untamed. On her left wrist, she wore the braided bracelet that now contained six pearls, one for each of her birthdays since being stranded on the island.

Holt slept on the bottom bunk and didn't wake from her stealthy landing near him. Alex crawled under the covers on the bottom bunk, nestled against him from behind, and clung to his abdomen. Holt woke and patted her hand.

"You're up early," he teased in a warm, weary tone. "Even for you."

"I thought I'd get an early start and beat the morning rush hour traffic," she announced cheerfully. "Anything special you want for breakfast?"

"Hmm, yes," Holt announced while lazily dreaming. "I'd love some French toast with pineapple syrup and crisp bacon."

"Mangoes it is," she chirped while resting her head on his shoulder. "What are your plans?"

"Nine holes at the country club, brandy with the boys, and a little wild boar hunting," he replied and attempted to glance at her but was unable to meet her gaze. "Feel like joining me?"

Alex wrinkled her nose and cringed. He'd tried numerous times to con her into boar hunting with him, but she couldn't stomach the idea.

"No, thanks," she informed him. "I don't mind eating what you kill, but I don't care to see how it's done."

"What are your plans?" he asked while rolling onto his back so he could face her.

"I promised Monster we'd go swimming. You know how he loves the water," she replied cheerfully. "Maybe do a little sightseeing."

"Sounds like fun," he announced. "Maybe I'll join you later."

"As long as you promise you won't turn all science teacher on us," she teased then grinned. "Do you need anything before I leave?"

Holt smiled warmly and indicated his cheek. Alex smiled and kissed him.

"I'll be back before lunch," she announced cheerfully and sprang up from the bed.

"Late as usual, I'm sure," he remarked with a sigh. "Remember our deal. If you're late, you have to clean up after lunch."

She smiled in response then turned and hurried to the cabin door.

Chapter Twenty

Alex walked along the worn path in the woods while carrying a four-foot long bamboo pole. She heard the trees rustling nearby, appeared curious and looked around. The area was deathly silent and almost creepy. Despite her reservations, Alex continued along the path. She heard the rustling sound again. Something large silently dropped from the trees onto the path behind her and rose up threateningly. Alex sensed something.

Without looking behind her, she dropped to the ground, rolled, and popped up in a crouched position with her stick held defensively. The large, black creature stood an imposing six feet tall on its hind legs. Monster snarled while baring his large mouthful of razor sharp teeth. He cracked his six-foot long, bullwhip tail before pouncing on top of her. Alex used the stick horizontally to catch the two-hundred-pound creature, placed her foot to his belly, and tossed him over her, throwing him roughly to the ground.

Monster hit the ground, rolled, and was immediately back into attack position, now on all fours. He gurgled and cracked his tail. Alex spun toward him and twirled the stick above her head. Monster leaped onto her and tackled her to the ground, pinning her shoulders. As her pole flew from her hands, Monster snarled with his long teeth only inches from her face. Alex stared at the large teeth and laughed nervously.

"Okay, okay," she cried out, wincing in pain. "You win! Off!"

Monster jumped off her and scaled a nearby tree. Alex slowly stood with some stiffness, brushed off the dirt, and reclaimed her pole. The rustling sounds from the tree suddenly stopped. She heard a repetitive thumping. Alex looked around in panic then hurried to a nearby tree and quickly scaled it. She crouched in the crook of the tree while listening to movement along the path. Alex clung to her pole and watched the path wondering what had Monster on high alert.

Damon appeared with his machete strapped to his hip and his pack over his shoulder. He stopped and looked at the path where she and Monster had wrestled. Alex marveled at the handsome man, who hadn't changed much in over six years. His hair was still short in a businessman cut and not a hair out of place. He wore his seemingly freshly washed shirt with the first two buttons open, allowing her a generous view of a light coating of dark chest hair. Something about the sturdy, rugged man stirred strange feelings inside her.

Alex looked at Monster, who clung to a nearby tree facing upside down while watching Damon. Monster was almost statuesque. Alex looked back at Damon while he studied the attack scene. He straightened, scanned the area, and then continued along the path. Alex watched him until he was gone then looked at Monster. He gurgled softly. She climbed partway down the tree and jumped the last few feet.

"Where do you suppose he's heading?" she asked while leaning against the tree.

She heard movement within the tree above her. Monster crawled headfirst partway down the tree just inches from her face and stared at her. Alex smiled and pet his nose.

"You're right," she announced with a sly grin while nodding. "We should follow him."

Alex walked quietly along the path, stalking the strange man. Monster spun around on the tree, scurried back up it, and disappeared out of sight.

§

The large pond contained a cascading waterfall down the stone embankment along the back edge. Flowering plant life grew out of the stone embankment. Large rocks and lush foliage added to the tropical beauty of the area surrounding the pond. Damon walked past the pond to a large rock, seemingly with a mission in mind. Alex scurried up a nearby tree to keep an eye on the intruder invading *her* domain.

"What do you suppose he's up to?" she whispered to Monster.

Damon kneeled alongside the large rock and removed some foliage from the base. He casually tossed a snake aside then removed bottles filled with liquid and two bundled packages. He took several empty bottles from his pack and placed them in the small pit along with a couple of books, a bundle of clothing, a microscope, and a small, brown sack. He replaced the foliage, filled his pack, and slung it over his shoulder then left. Alex watched as he passed beneath her tree. She had to admit; his presence was a little odd.

Chapter Twenty-one

Later that afternoon, Alex hurried across the clearing and into the lighthouse. She was late for lunch as usual, and it was almost to be expected. Monster leaped from a nearby tree, onto the side of the lighthouse, and scurried up the side to the top, entering through a missing window. Alex set her bamboo pole alongside the door next to Holt's pole and approached Holt by the fire pit. He turned a slab of meat on the open fire while reading a book. Since he was never ready on time anymore, it would appear as if he'd gotten used to her being late

"Anything exciting this morning?" he asked without looking up from his book.

Alex removed the iron kettle from above the pit with use of a cloth. She poured hot water over a strainer with crushed tea leaves then poured the tea into two cups.

"That guy was prowling around our area again," she informed him.

Holt cast a glance at her and appeared curious. "Oh? Did he see you?"

"Of course not," she announced proudly. "Monster taught me how to blend with the scenery."

Holt chuckled. "So you hid in a tree?"

Alex sneered at his teasing remark.

"Lunch will be ready soon," he informed her. "Did you wash up?"

"Yes, right before we came back," she replied then eyed the book in his hand. "Is that a new book?"

"Oh, yes," he replied cheerfully. "I found a few things on my hunting trip this morning."

Holt nodded to the bench, indicating the things he'd found. Alex approached the table and eyed the small pile of clothing. She suspiciously looked at Holt as he removed the meat on the spit from the fire. He placed it on a large, metal platter on the table. Alex eyed the second book on the pile. She wouldn't have believed it if she hadn't seen it, although the two bundles and the microscope were missing. He'd been trading with the interloper! Holt passed Alex a plate with a slab of boar meat along with a knife and fork and sat at the end of the table near her with his plate.

"Where do you find all of this great stuff?" she remarked, hoping to get the truth from him. "I never find anything good on my walks."

"Maybe that's because I spend more time looking at the ground than you."

"I guess I need to be a little more observant and maybe I'll find things too," she remarked.

"Want to go clamming this afternoon?"

"Yeah, sure," she chirped enthusiastically. "Monster loves clamming."

"He's got the toes for it."

She eyed him slyly and grinned. "Then maybe afterward we could practice a little."

"I'm still sore from yesterday's practice," he informed her.

"Exactly why you need to practice," she teased and hid her smile.

"You're like a little jungle ninja," he scoffed under his breath. "I don't see how kicking the crap out of me is going to make you any better."

"You used to love teaching me karate and making me practice," she insisted.

"That was back when I was the one doing the tossing," he replied and eyed her while raising a clever brow. "I'm getting old. I don't bounce like I used to."

Alex glanced at him with some concern. "Are you feeling okay?"

"Just a little tired."

"I'll give you a massage tonight," Alex announced. "You'll feel better."

Chapter Twenty-two

It was late afternoon, and the sun was shining on the small, secluded beach. Alex and Holt were knee-deep in the clear water while digging for clams with their toes. Monster had his head underwater as his claws dug wildly into the sand at the bottom, causing water to splash all around him. Alex and Holt watched Monster bodysurf to the beach then hurl up nearly a dozen clams. He leaped back into the water, swam toward them, and again started blasting into the sand. Alex and Holt exchanged looks and shook their heads.

An hour or two later, Monster lay on the beach with dozens of clams in front of him as well as dozens of empty shells. He pried them open with his teeth and claws and ate out the raw centers while Holt and Alex performed karate moves on each other. Holt flipped Alex over his hip and celebrated like a linebacker scoring a goal. Alex lay in the sand and stared at him, shaking her head at his celebration.

§

Evening had arrived, and the area surrounding the lighthouse was dark. Holt lay face down on his bunk while Alex sat on the edge of the bed and dug her palms into his back and shoulders. He gasped slightly and half looked at her.

"Who taught you to be so rough?" he demanded with his face into the mattress.

"I believe you did," she teased while grinning. "I have to get the knots out. You really need to let me do this more often. Your back is so tight; I could bounce a quarter off it."

"It's coming back to me why I don't let you give me massages," he muttered.

"Big baby."

Monster crept along the ceiling from the lighthouse stairs and slowly approached the top bunk. It creaked loudly as he nestled into Alex's bed.

She eyed the bunk above them and held back her laugh. "He thinks we don't know he's there."

"That's because he thinks he's a poodle."

Alex crawled over Holt, straddled his thighs, and began massaging the top of his shoulders.

Holt suddenly tensed to her on top of him. "Uh, new technique?"

"I get sore from twisting," she replied simply. "This works better."

Holt remained tense, unable to relax. "If you're sore, you should stop."

"No, I'm fine now."

"I'm not sure I am," he remarked.

"Is the sheet too tight?" she questioned.   "Should I remove it?"

"God no!"

She stopped massaging him and stared at his bare back. "What's wrong?"

"Can you please just get off me?" he practically demanded.   "I'd prefer you didn't do that."

Alex uncertainly moved off him and sat on the edge of the bed while staring at him.   Holt didn't move, and it concerned her.

"What's wrong?"

"I'm just tired," he remarked gently.

Alex continued to stare at him not certain she believed him.   "Oh, okay," she gently remarked then moved from the bunk.

Holt still didn't move, which seemed odd.   Had she hurt him?   Why wouldn't he just say she had?   His behavior seemed odd lately.

"I'll, uh, be upstairs in the lighthouse if you need anything," she remarked timidly.

Holt gave her a slight wave without moving from his position on the lower bed.   Alex frowned and headed for the stairs.

Chapter Twenty-three

Two o'clock in the morning. Alex tossed within the top bunk having a difficult time falling asleep after her bizarre interaction with Holt that evening. She felt the bunk shaking, which only happened when Monster was climbing around, but she was certain he was still upstairs. Alex climbed from her bunk to investigate. Within the bottom bed, Holt shivered violently beneath the covers. Alex sat on the bunk and gently touched his shoulder. He was cold and clammy to the touch.

"Holt? Are you okay?"

"I'm freezing," he chattered softly.

She didn't understand how he was freezing when it wasn't that cold. It was actually a moderately warm night. Alex immediately grabbed her blanket from the top bunk and placed it over him. He still shivered. She touched his forehead, appeared concerned, and quickly climbed under the covers with him. She held him against her while he shook and attempted to keep him warm. He clung to her for her warmth.

§

Early the following morning, Alex woke to the sun poking through the wooden window shutters. She remained in the bottom bunk the rest of the night and turned over to check on Holt. He faced her while sleeping peacefully. At least he'd stopped shivering. Alex gently touched his arm. She suddenly gasped with concern and felt his head.

She pulled her hand away in surprise. "Holt, you're burning up!"

There was no response. Alex lightly nudged him. He still didn't wake. She hovered over him and again attempted to wake him.

"Holt, are you okay? Please, wake up," she pleaded softly with concern. "I don't know what I'm supposed to do."

An hour later, Alex sat in the lower bed with her knees to her chest and watched Holt, who still didn't wake or move. She wiped the tears from her face and allowed her head to fall back against the bedpost. Alex knew she needed to do something, but she wasn't sure what that was. She stared at Holt several minutes longer, sniffed, and leaned over him.

"I'll be back, I promise," she whispered.

Alex kissed his excessively hot forehead and jumped from the bed. She hurried to the door and snatched her pole on the way out.

Alex hurried through the south woods with her pole firmly grasped in her hands. Monster was heard rustling in the trees not far from her, following her from above. She approached the stream where Damon had stitched her leg over six years earlier and looked around.

"Come on," she muttered while scanning the area. "Where are you?"

Alex fought her tears, unable to control her emotions. Monster climbed partway down the tree and gurgled, as if sensing her fear. Alex looked at the path to the forbidden woods before her. Her look hardened, and she hurried along the path into the forbidden territory. Alex continued along the path with Monster following from the trees.

She'd traveled a long distance before hearing the unusual sound of metal clanging. Monster hung off a wall of vegetation covering an old, chain-link fence. The twenty-foot tall fence appeared to extend forever. Alex followed the path along the fence to an opening. Monster's tail thumped against a tree trunk. Alex barely looked around before scaling a nearby tree while clinging to her pole.

"Go to hell, you fucking moron," a familiar male voice shouted in anger.

Damon appeared from the opening with his machete attached to his hip and his pack over his shoulder. He walked along the path and past Alex's tree. She was momentarily conflicted by what she should do then took a deep breath and jumped from the tree. She landed softly in a crouched position several feet behind Damon with the pole securely in her hands.

Despite her soft landing, Damon must've heard her. He spun around while unsheathing his machete and took a threatening stance. Alex skillfully twirled her pole and took her own fighting stance. She stood statuesque with her eyes locked on Damon. He stared at her with surprise and lowered the machete.

"What the hell are you doing here?" he cried out in a whisper then adamantly shook his head while casting looks around him. "You can't be here! Go. Before someone sees you!"

Alex remained in her fighting stance with a fixed gaze upon him. Uncontrollable tears streaked her face. Despite years of fear and distrust, she had to risk it. She slowly lowered the pole and straightened.

"Holt won't wake up. I don't know what to do," she informed him in a soft tone. "It might be a brain aneurysm. Please help him."

They heard male voices near the fence. Damon looked at the fence with alarm then back at Alex. "You need to go," he growled.

"Not without you."

Damon stared at her only a moment, ran his fingers through his hair, and then frowned. "I'll be five minutes behind you. They can't see you," he insisted then pointed down the path with hostility. "Now go."

She heard thumping against the tree, alarming her. Alex moved past Damon without turning her back on him then ran along the path. Damon looked around then hurried after her. As Damon followed her from several feet behind, Alex couldn't help her feelings of distrust and nervous anxiety being in close proximity to the man she'd been told to avoid.

Alex attempted to keep an eye on him while keeping her distance from him. She'd been taught to distrust him and was told he wasn't their ally, yet Holt had been trading with him for quite some time. She had to be able to trust him. She had nowhere else to turn. Holt needed help, and she needed Damon.

Chapter Twenty-four

Alex entered the lighthouse and hurried to Holt's bedside. Holt was in the same position when she left a couple of hours earlier. Alex kneeled by the bed and gently touched his face. He was still burning up with fever. Damon entered the lighthouse a few seconds behind her. Alex straightened and immediately backed away from the bed, keeping her distance from the questionable man. Damon sat on the edge of the bunk and examined Holt's condition. Alex remained tense for several reasons and watched with concern.

"He has a fever," he informed her then eyed her. "Did he complain about feeling bad?"

She clung to her pole in one hand and insecurely rubbed her chilled arm with the other. "He complained about being tired all day," she announced and shivered slightly. "In the middle of the night, he said he was freezing."

"Are you feeling sick?"

"A little," she replied while nervously choking on her words. "Why?"

"It would be easy to ingest something toxic," he informed her.

"No, he knows every plant out there," she insisted. "He wouldn't make a mistake." She felt her entire body tremble with fear. "Will he be okay? Is it a brain aneurysm?"

Damon looked at her with surprise. "What?" he asked then shook his head. "No, it's probably the flu. Get some cold water from the stream."

Alex was relieved that Damon didn't think it was a brain aneurysm, but she remained concerned over Holt's condition anyway. She grabbed a bucket and hurried from the lighthouse.

§

Damon remained sitting on the edge of the bed nearly half an hour later. Holt had cold cloths on his forehead, under his neck, and under his armpits. Alex watched with nervous anticipation, having set her pole down in order to pace and insecurely rub her shoulders. Damon removed a bottle of pills from his pack and approached her. She took a step back to keep distance between them. He set the bottle on the table.

"Once the fever breaks, he'll come around," Damon informed her. "Change the cloths every twenty minutes or so to help keep him cool. When he's responsive, give him two fever reducers every four hours. Make sure he drinks plenty of water." He hesitated and seemed to consider his next comment carefully. "I'll come back tomorrow and check on him."

Alex's eyes widened, and she nearly lunged at him. "You're leaving?"

"He should be fine in a few hours," Damon insisted then eyed her. "I'd think you'd be grateful to get rid of me."

"No, please don't go. If something happens to him--" She hesitated while staring into Damon's eyes. "He's all that matters to me."

Damon set his pack down and groaned. "Great. I'm officially a nursemaid." He eyed Alex and raised his brows almost demandingly. "I realize you don't get much company, but it's customary to offer tea."

Alex exhaled and managed a tiny, nervous smile. "Yes, of course."

While Alex prepared tea, Damon took it upon himself to explore the cabin. He looked inside the small pantry near the fire pit and appeared intrigued by what he'd found among the fully stocked shelves.

"Wow, this guy's a regular Martha Stewart," Damon remarked. "Homemade soap, candles--" He then opened a glass jar and sniffed it. "What's this stuff?"

"Boar jerky," she replied. "Help yourself."

Damon ate some jerky and groaned his approval. "Damn, that's good." He ate a few more pieces then shut the pantry door.

Alex set a cup of tea on the table for him and moved away from it. She took her own cup and sat on the edge of the table while keeping her attention on Holt in the bed. Damon picked up his cup and sat on the table several feet away.

"He's turned this old place into quite the little love nest, hasn't he?" Damon announced.

She eyed him with confusion then realized what he'd insinuated. "I think you've got the wrong idea," Alex insisted.

"Just the two of you *alone* for the last six years?" He chuckled in his throat. "I think I have the right idea. No normal, healthy man can live alongside a young, attractive woman as his only company for six years and not have a sexual relationship with her."

Alex stared at him with surprise as a thousand thoughts raced through her mind. "Would that make him get sick like that?" she suddenly gasped. "Is that why this happened?"

It was Damon's turn to stare. "You're kidding, right?" he boldly announced. "If lack of sex caused illness, half the men in the world would suddenly drop dead." He then considered the comment and smirked. "That is, providing they hadn't gone blind first."

She frowned while staring at the look on his face. "You're mocking me."

He suddenly chuckled in his throat. "Yes, I'm mocking you, because that's the craziest thing I've ever heard." He fell silent a moment while studying her as his look turned serious. "How old are you?"

"Twenty-two last month. Why?"

He snorted a laugh and nodded. "Oh--that explains a lot."

"What does it explain?"

"Your childlike innocence," Damon replied then appeared curious. "So he's never tried to hook-up with you?"

"He doesn't think of me that way," she replied and raised her brow with a curious look. "Why is that so hard to believe?"

"Because he's a man."

"Well, he's not that kind of man," she scoffed, quickly becoming annoyed with him.

"I hate to burst your bubble, but after six years of abstaining, all men are 'that kind of man'," he teased. "You just don't want to admit that Holt has needs like every other man."

"He would have no reason to keep his needs from me. I would do anything for him, and he knows that," she informed him sharply. "If he wanted a sexual relationship, we'd be in one. It's that simple."

Damon stared at her with surprise then muttered, "Fucker certainly sets the bar high for the rest of us poor bastards."

Chapter Twenty-five

When evening finally came, Alex again changed the cool compresses on Holt's body and gently touched his face. He didn't feel as hot as he had, so the cool cloths were working. She leaned down and kissed his cheek, relieved he was doing better, although she wished he would wake up. The cabin was now dimly lit with several candles placed strategically around the room. Alex looked across the cabin at Damon, who sat in the chair by the fire pit with his feet propped on the nearby bench while watching her with Holt. His interest was puzzling. She wondered what he was thinking. Maybe she didn't want to know. She wasn't sure.

"I think his fever is coming down," she informed him. "He doesn't feel as hot."

She approached the table while studying Damon and uncertainly sat on the bench near his feet.

"I'm sorry for keeping you here so late," she announced timidly while fidgeting. "I can't tell you how much I appreciate what you've done."

"I didn't do anything," he replied simply with little concern.

"That's a matter of opinion," she remarked then hesitated feeling insecure. "If there's anything I can do to repay you--"

Damon studied her, appeared tense, and straightened. "Don't turn all girly on me now," he remarked wearily. "I'm tired and not thinking straight."

"You aren't going to go back to your camp anymore tonight, are you?"

"No," he replied with a sigh, "but I might go to the beach and get some sleep."

"Take the upper bunk," she insisted. "I'm going to stay with Holt anyway."

He gave her a strange look. "Are you sure?"

Alex stood and nodded now offering a more sincere smile. Damon walked past Alex toward the bunk. For the first time, she didn't flinch as he passed her. Although it was only a small thing, he seemed to notice she was less tense now. Damon pulled the cover back on the top bunk. Monster lifted his large, black head, looked directly at Damon, and hissed. Damon cried out, jumped backward, and collided with Alex.

Before she could even react or speak, he pulled her halfway across the room with him and reached for his machete on the table. She was possibly more startled by the way he grabbed and held her than his panic-stricken reaction. Alex grabbed his wrist and stopped him from grabbing the weapon.

"It's okay," she cried out. "It's just Monster."

Damon cast a look at her as if not understanding a word she said then stared at the creature on the top bunk.

"What?" he gasped and again attempted to reach his machete.

Alex refused to release his arm and held him back. "He's my pet," she cried out. "Don't hurt him."

"What?" he again proclaimed and now looked at her with surprise. "Your pet? What the hell--?"

Damon looked at Monster on the top bunk. In the dim lighting, he was barely seen. He gurgled and nestled back into the bunk, although he was obviously watching Damon.

"I didn't know he was in the bunk, I swear," she insisted. "He's harmless."

Damon looked at Alex with surprise, his eyes meeting hers from only inches away as he held her against him in his attempt to protect her from her pet. When he realized the way he held her body pressed against his, his expression suddenly changed, and he moaned in response.

"Oh, hell--"

He put his hand on her neck and placed his lips against hers, kissing her passionately and aggressively on the mouth. Alex tensed with surprise to his aggressive kiss. A thousand thoughts raced through her mind in those few seconds. Her heart was racing and a strange ache swept through her entire body.

The first and only time she'd been kissed was when Bronson attacked her, but this was nothing like that. She feared she enjoyed it, but that wasn't possible. She didn't trust him. She couldn't enjoy the kiss of some man she didn't know and didn't trust. Could she? He broke off the kiss and practically jumped away from her.

"I'm sorry," he quickly announced while seeming flustered. "I should--" He stumbled over his words while fidgeting. "I need to go."

Damon hurried from the lighthouse, not even taking time to grab his pack or his machete. Alex watched him bolt from the cabin with surprise. She had no idea what had just happened. He kissed her. Why was he so upset? Once he was out the door, she gently placed her fingers to her lips still feeling his passionate kiss. The phantom sensation was almost as pleasurable as the original kiss had been.

"Wow," she muttered.

Once she collected herself, Alex returned to the bottom bunk and placed fresh compresses on Holt's body. He finally woke and looked at her with disorientation.

"Hey," he muttered.

Alex stared at him with relief and took his hand in hers while attempting to contain her smile. She had her doubts he'd ever wake despite Damon's conviction.

"How are you feeling?"

"Pretty shitty, thanks for asking," he replied then made a face. "Why am I wet?"

"You had a high fever," she replied. "We were trying to bring it down with cool compresses."

Holt appeared disoriented and was fixated on his damp sheets. "How long was I out?"

"All day," she informed him then recalled her instructions. "You're supposed to drink lots of water and take some pills every four hours."

He was oddly silent a moment while staring at her. "Pills? What happened?" Holt asked as his eyes widened. She could see the color drain from his face. "What did you do?"

"Nothing."

Damon entered the lighthouse with a guilty look on his face and immediately fidgeted. "I, uh, forgot--"

Holt saw him, shut his eyes, and groaned almost painfully. "No, Alex, you didn't."

Damon approached the bunk and glanced at his recovering patient.

Holt opened his eyes, stared at Damon, and again groaned. He immediately shifted his attention to Alex. "How long has he been here?"

"Since late morning," Alex replied. "You were unresponsive. I didn't know what else to do."

"Please tell me you didn't go to the south side of the island," Holt gasped.

She stared at him with surprise, not thinking he'd be so opposed considering the situation. "I had to. You needed help."

"I'd better go," Damon muttered.

"No, it's dark out," Alex announced while looking back at him. "You shouldn't be wandering around the woods in the dark."

"Alex, he should go," Holt informed her.

She glared at Holt where he remained lying in bed. "No, he's staying. You're too sick to argue." Alex stood and looked at Monster in her upper bunk. "Monster, upstairs."

Monster bared his teeth at her in protest, scaled the wall, and ran along the ceiling to the lighthouse.

Damon stared wide-eyed at the large creature until it was gone, witnessing its full size. "Christ," he gasped in near shock.

Alex looked back at Damon and indicated the top bunk. "There's your bunk."

Damon eyed Holt and smirked slyly. "Never argue with a woman," he announced then pulled himself onto the upper bunk and made himself comfortable.

Holt managed to sit up within the lower bunk. "Alex, you don't understand--"

"No, Holt, *you* don't understand," she snapped back surprising him.

Holt attempted to stand despite her protest. Ultimately, she was forced to help him to his feet.

"I'll put dry sheets on your bed," she announced and gave him a stern look. "You'd better take some of those pills and drink some water."

"I need to use the men's room," he muttered then weakly headed for the door.

"Do you need help?" she questioned with concern for his stability on his feet.

"Even if I do, I'll manage," he barked a little too quickly, oddly annoyed with her.

Damon snickered from the top bunk.

"Shut up," Holt snarled then left the lighthouse.

Damon moved onto his elbow from his position on the upper bunk and looked at Alex, who stood just a little below eye level. "You said you owed me for today," he announced. "Don't tell Holt I kissed you, and we'll call it even. Okay?"

Chapter Twenty-six

Alex woke early the following morning within the bottom bunk and felt Holt sleeping peacefully against her from behind with his arm securely around her waist. Alex affectionately placed her hand on his arm and tried not to disturb him. He nuzzled her neck and pressed against her backside. Alex suddenly tensed and rolled onto her back. Holt groaned in his sleep then opened his eyes. He saw Alex, appeared alarmed, realizing where he was, and jumped away from her. He gasped with surprise then nervously ran his fingers through his mussed hair while on his back.

"Sorry, I was somewhere else," he groaned while appearing ashamed of his actions.

"It's okay," she replied with little concern to the incident. "It's not the first time you thought you were somewhere else."

Holt stared at her with surprise and partially turned to face her. "What?"

"It's okay," she insisted with little concern. "That's all that matters."

Holt lay on his back and groaned with shame. "Please tell me--" He pointed to the upper bunk.

"He left a few minutes ago."

He closed his eyes and groaned. "Thank God."

"Christ!" Damon was heard yelling from outside sounding panicked. "Alex!"

Alex sprang from the bed, grabbed her fighting pole, and ran outside. She only ran a few feet from the cabin when she saw Damon standing near the woods before Monster. Monster stood on his hind legs, towering over Damon while staring him in the eyes with his teeth bared in a threatening manner.

"Bad, Monster!" she screamed while running toward them.

Upon hearing her voice, Monster moved onto all fours and spun around. He purposely whipped his tail, knocking Damon's feet out from under him. Damon was thrown to the ground and landed harshly on his back. Alex kneeled alongside him as Monster scurried into the woods and climbed up a tree.

"Are you okay?" she gasped.

"That monster doesn't like me," he muttered while pulling himself into a sitting position and rubbing his sore body parts before standing.

"He can be quite territorial."

Damon brushed himself off and eyed her with a curious look. "Over you?"

"What? No," she announced, finding the comment almost humorous. "You slept in my bed. He probably thought your scent didn't belong there." Her eyes then widened with an afterthought. "Oh, and very important." She indicated a nearby tree and smiled nervously. "That tree with all the scratches is his. I suggest you don't mark it. He *really* doesn't like that."

Damon stared at her a moment as his eyes widened with realization. "Oh," he muttered nervously. "I think I know why he hates me."

She groaned and shook her head. "You're lucky," she remarked with concern. "He could have sprayed you like he did Holt."

He stared at her with some surprise. "Yeah, I'm getting out of here before that happens," Damon announced and grabbed his discarded pack.

Alex managed a timid smile while staring at him. "Thanks again for everything."

Damon snorted a laugh while attempting to relax after his run-in with Monster. "Yeah, see you around."

She watched him walk away then hid her smile while admiring the handsome man.

Chapter Twenty-seven

Later that morning, Alex brought a cup of tea to Holt and joined him on the lower bunk. He looked much better, although he remained slightly pale and weak.

"You should probably take it easy for a couple of days," she informed him while handing him his tea. "You need to work on getting your strength back. I can take care of everything."

"More advice from the witch doctor?"

"I know you don't approve of what I did--"

"No, Alex. It's partially my fault," he replied with a sigh. "When we ran into Damon six years ago, he told me about this place for shelter. He also told me why we needed to stay away from his camp." He stared at her a moment and appeared moderately tense. "It's not a camp. It's a prison." Holt fidgeted while staring at her. "There was some incident that wiped out nearly everyone. What remains are thirty-some hard-core convicts with no guards and no locked doors. Thirty men who are murderers and rapists."

Alex stared at Holt with alarm. She could almost feel her entire body twitching at the thought. "And you thought it was a good idea to keep this information to yourself?"

"According to him, the others rarely leave the prison grounds," he informed her and shifted uncomfortably. "Most of them want nothing to do with the jungle. As long as we stay on the north side, they'll never know we exist."

"And which type of convict is Damon?" she asked with some concern.

"He's not a rapist, I asked. I believe him when he says he's not," Holt informed her. "He intended to take us to the prison for shelter until he saw you. He was concerned for your safety." He inhaled a deep, nervous breath. "You not only went to the south side, but he was here the entire day with you."

"And he had every opportunity to hurt me, but he didn't," she replied.

"He may not be a rapist, but he did something to earn his place in that prison," Holt responded. "Our deal was he didn't have any contact with you."

"That's my fault, but since the two of you have been exchanging goods, I assumed he would help," she informed him.

Holt stared at her with surprise. "You know about that?" he gasped.

"I saw him hiding things at the pond," she reluctantly admitted. "Later that day, you showed up with the things he'd left."

"He was nice enough to leave things for us, so I started leaving things for him," Holt informed her. "Our face-to-face meetings were minimal, but that doesn't make him someone I trust with you. Promise me you'll stay away from him."

"Okay, I'll stay away from him," she replied then hesitated and considered something that troubled her. She fidgeted slightly. "He said something last night that concerned me."

"I can only imagine what he said," Holt muttered under his breath.

"He said it's physically impossible for us to be the way we are, because all men have needs including you," she announced.

Holt stared at her with surprise then frowned. "I'm going to kill him," he snarled then met her gaze. "It's complicated, Alex."

"Complicated?" she gasped with surprise, unable to look away from him. "He wasn't wrong?"

"It's not as black and white as he makes it sound," Holt insisted. "When we met, you were fifteen. You became like a daughter to me. We've been together, just the two of us, for six years. That can cause sexual tensions for any man." He fidgeted slightly. "I admit, there are moments when I'm reminded that you're a sexually desirable young woman, and sometimes when you feel the need to cling to me, it triggers that response." He drew a deep breath then offered a timid smile. "They're not feelings I would ever act upon, but like with that massage, it's sometimes difficult to will away that response."

"Is that why you seemed upset?"

"It's not your fault," he explained. "You didn't know your actions could be considered sexual."

She sank into thought then eyed him. "Karate practice?"

"You tend to pin me down in a sexually compromising position, but I've been guilty of allowing you to do it," he informed her then immediately raised a brow. "Basically, you should avoid straddling most parts of a man's body. It affects brain activity."

"Oh--" Alex considered the comment, placed her hand on his lower arm, and timidly looked into his eyes. "You know I'd do anything for you, Holt," she announced gently. "If you have needs to fulfill, you know I'll do whatever you want."

Holt appeared shocked then looked away and groaned while placing his hand on his forehead. "Oh, God." He fidgeted, looked back at her, and took her hand. "This goes beyond my sexual needs, Alex. I want to keep looking at you like my daughter. If I did anything to destroy that, I'd hate myself."

"I like our relationship the way it is too. I'm glad we got this out into the open," she replied and offered a warm smile. "Now you can tell me so I know to stop, although you're not getting out of karate practice because I enjoy tossing you around."

He laughed. "Yeah, I kind of like knocking you on your ass too."

Alex and Holt laughed and held each other in an affectionate embrace. She then pulled away and eyed him with a curious look.

"So what was in the bottles?"

"Excuse me?"

"Damon took out full bottles and put in empty ones," she informed him. "What was in them?"

"Moonshine," Holt reluctantly replied. "I have a distillery east of the pond."

She stared at him with surprise and hid her smile. "You naughty bootlegger."

"He claims it makes the guys at the prison more tolerable when they're buzzed," Holt informed her. "That and cigarettes."

"You're making cigarettes too?"

"No, I just grow and dry the tobacco. They roll their own," he replied. "Damon brings me a lot of useful things twice a week. A lot of what I do around here is because he brought me the proper tools."

"Yeah, he loved your boar jerky."

Holt's expression dropped. "No, you didn't let him see that." He groaned and shook his head. "He was probably snooping around to see what else I could make for him."

Chapter Twenty-eight

The pond area was peaceful on the warm afternoon. A few days had passed since Holt's fever broke, and Alex finally felt comfortable enough to leave him alone for more than a few hours while she got out of the cabin for some fresh air. Alex sat in the crook of a tree eight feet from the ground with one leg dangling from the branch and a book open in her hand. She was supposed to be reading the book, but her mind was anywhere but within the pages. She'd been feeling distracted the last few days, and she wasn't even sure why.

Monster lay across a branch further up from her with all four legs dangling. Despite that he appeared to be asleep, his long tail snaked down the tree and poked her in the side. She jumped with surprise and looked around.

Monster pulled his tail away and still appeared to be asleep. Alex eyed the creature then smirked.

"Sneak."

Monster suddenly curled his legs up beneath him and stared toward the path with a frozen look. His tail thumped the tree, alerting her to something. Alex looked at the path and saw Damon approaching the area near them. Alex gave Monster the quiet sign. Damon entered the clearing and approached the 'exchange' rock just beyond her tree. He again removed bottles and packages from the hidden pit and replaced them with empty bottles, laboratory equipment, food items, and a few more books.

He wiped the sweat from his forehead then removed his shirt and shoes. Alex appeared curious and wondered what he was doing. When he removed his pants, Alex placed her hand to her mouth and held back her gasp. She'd officially seen her first naked man! Despite their close quarters, Alex had never even seen Holt naked, so she caught herself staring at the unclothed man with more than curious interest. She watched as Damon dove into the water then looked at Monster on his elevated branch from hers.

"Don't tell Holt what we just saw."

Monster bared his teeth in something resembling a grin and hissed almost as if laughing. Alex stared at the large creature with a slightly stunned look.

"Oh, my God, you're grinning, aren't you?" she gasped then glared at him through squinting eyes. "I knew you understood what I was saying."

Alex looked back at the pond and watched Damon swimming within the water. She'd been interested in boys back when she attended school in her previous life, but she never understood the big deal. After a few minutes of watching Damon, she found herself admiring his moderately muscular shoulders and chest. Something strange stirred inside her. He was only in the pond for a little more than ten minutes before returning to shore and his discarded clothing. Despite knowing it was wrong, Alex leaned forward and watched as he slipped back into his pants. She couldn't seem to take her eyes off his manly parts until they disappeared beneath his pants. She couldn't deny she was disappointed.

Monster's tail thumped the tree, catching Damon's attention. As he turned to locate the sound, Damon was punched in the face by a man Alex had never seen before. She then saw a second unfamiliar man grab Damon's machete. Arnold and Dennis were slightly grungy looking men in their late thirties. They wore wrinkled, soiled clothing, and it appeared as if neither man bathed or shaved in days. Their hair was unkempt and scraggly, unlike Damon's neatly trimmed hair.

"You've made your last trade, Damon," Arnold announced while sneering at him through grimy teeth. "We're taking over."

Dennis grabbed Damon's discarded pack, opened it, and grinned in response. "He made the exchange," he announced. "His contact must make the drop then return later."

"We can wait," Arnold replied with a sinister grin. "We've got nothing but time."

"He's an old, island native. He won't deal with you," Damon snarled while glaring at the two men. "Go back before you ruin everything."

"I don't think so," Arnold announced while chuckling. "No more rationing hooch and smokes. I'm sure he can make more with the proper motivation. Some of us want to get drunk at night. Make this rock livable."

Monster leaped from his branch to a nearby tree just a few feet away, causing the branches to sway. Both men looked up at the moving branches with some alarm. Damon lunged for Arnold and the machete. Arnold turned his head just in time and swung the weapon for Damon. Damon dove to the ground to avoid the blade but was a little too slow. The machete struck a bamboo pole.

Arnold appeared surprised with the connection and stared at Alex holding her fighting pole. She clutched her pole and stared at him with an emotionless glare. Once the initial surprise wore off, Dennis grinned and laughed.

"Holy hell," Dennis cried out with enthusiasm. "He has himself a woman!"

Alex pulled her pole back as Damon jumped to his feet near her. She maintained her cold stare, skillfully twirled the pole, and moved into an attack stance. Her eyes were locked on Arnold holding the machete.

"Oh, she's in attack position," Damon announced while playing up the hostile woman angle. "You'd better drop the machete. She has trust issues."

"We want her alive, man," Dennis said while cackling with delight. "Don't injure her too seriously."

"I mean it, Arnold," Damon snarled. "Drop the weapon and back off."

"Are you kidding?" Dennis cried out while laughing at the comment. "A live woman is worth more than a whole distillery."

Damon leaned closer to Alex and whispered in her ear. "Give me the stick and run."

She didn't flinch at his comment. Dennis lunged for Alex in an attempt to disarm her without hurting her, since they obviously wanted her alive. She twirled the bamboo pole and struck him repeatedly with amazing skill and speed. Dennis cried out and jumped with each strike, unable to stop the thrashing. Arnold, who'd had enough, slashed at her with the machete. Alex spun around, blocking the blade, and threw his arm upward. She followed through with a foot to his chest, kicking him away from her.

As he stumbled backward, Alex knocked the machete from his hand. She slashed with the pole in the opposite direction, snapping him to the right then spun into a high roundhouse kick, and struck him in the face. As he fell to the ground, Alex landed gracefully, spun into a roll, and knocked Dennis's feet out from under him with the bamboo pole. She flipped completely through and sprang back to her feet.

Alex twirled the pole above her head in one hand then returned to her attack position and watched both men now on the ground. Both men recovered, now a little wiser, jumped to their feet, and simultaneously lunged for her. Alex pummeled Arnold repeatedly with the pole while kicking Dennis. Arnold grabbed Alex's pole with both hands, stopping her assault on Dennis, allowing Dennis the opportunity to grab her from behind. She used Dennis's body for support and kicked Arnold in the chest with both feet.

As Arnold flew backward, Alex landed on the ground with Dennis still holding her from behind. She cracked Dennis on the side of the head with the pole, forcing him to release her, and then spun toward him. He was about to lunge for her when Damon grabbed him from behind and effortlessly snapped his neck. Alex saw the fatal blow, took a step back, and stared with surprise. She was momentarily thrown off her game.

Damon leaped to the ground, snatched his machete, and threw it past Alex. Alex spun to see the machete impale Arnold in the abdomen. Arnold clutched the machete handle with horror as blood spilled out around the blade, and he collapsed to the ground. Alex looked at Damon with her mouth hanging open and shock on her face. He casually walked past her and pulled his machete from Arnold's lifeless body. Alex returned to her attack position now directed at Damon but remained horrified and confused.

"You killed them!" she cried out while staring at him. "They were unarmed!"

"They're killers, Alex," he casually informed her. "You don't wait until they're armed to take them out. They wanted me dead and you as their personal sex toy." He sharply raised his brows. "And when Holt arrived, they would have killed him too. Judge me if you must, but they had to go."

Alex remained in attack position a moment longer then relaxed and straightened. "He warned me about you," she gasped while shaking her head. "I should have known he was right. He's always right."

"Was Bronson armed when Holt killed him?" Damon asked while raising a clever brow.

Alex stared at Damon with surprise, uncertain how to respond, and then looked away. "I misspoke," she announced timidly. "I'm sorry."

"Trust me; I'm used to it."

Monster climbed down his tree, slinked quietly toward Dennis' body, and sniffed it.

Alex saw him near the body and gasped with surprise. "Monster, no!"

Monster hissed then scurried back up his tree.

Damon grabbed his shirt from the nearby rock and slipped into it. "Yeah, we don't want him developing a taste for human flesh," he remarked.

She suddenly cringed. "Oh, that's disgusting."

"Keep him from eating that one while I dispose of this one," Damon instructed. "It's a good twenty minutes to the bluffs and back."

Damon left with Arnold's lifeless body. Alex sat on a nearby rock and stared at the dead man. She couldn't believe the thoughts racing through her mind at that moment. She couldn't process what had just happened. Could killing them be justified? Holt appeared in the clearing, saw the dead man, and hurried for Alex. He pulled her into his arms and away from the body.

"What happened?" he asked and immediately scanned her for injuries. "Did that man hurt you?"

She pulled away from him, stared into his eyes, and put on a brave front for his sake. "Two men jumped Damon," she informed him. "I intervened, and Damon killed them."

Holt stared at her a moment as if not understanding a word she said. "Are you okay?"

"Yeah, I'm okay," she replied and managed a tiny smile. "They were bad men." She indicated the dead man not far from them. "*That* one was overly enthusiastic to meet me."

Holt's look turned cold as his eyes narrowed. "Remind me to thank Damon."

"I was a little hard on him," she informed Holt. "I didn't expect him to kill them so swiftly like that. I mean, I understand his logic, but it was just unsettling. I'm not sure how I feel about what happened."

"We're in a lawless land filled with very evil men," Holt informed her while gently touching her shoulder as he stared into her eyes. "I guess he's hardened to it, but that doesn't make him wrong."

"I know," she replied while remaining deep in thought. She understood, but she just wanted to make the images go away.

Chapter Twenty-nine

Later that day, Alex sat on the beach while insecurely clinging to her knees and watched the tide as it crashed to shore then gently rolled out again. Monster sunned himself on a large rock while on his back with all four feet in the air and his long tail dangling limply to the ground. When Alex heard someone approach, she looked back and saw Damon appear on the beach. She avoided looking at him as he joined her on the white sand.

"I thought you went home," she remarked.

"Holt was in a talkative mood," Damon replied with little emotion. "I think he's concerned that we were meeting secretly. He'd probably be distraught if he knew you'd been in the tree the whole time."

She immediately felt her cheeks redden and turned defensive while casting a quick look at him. "I wasn't spying," she insisted. "I was reading."

"I'm sure that's the case," he casually replied, although it was possible he didn't believe her. "I'm sorry I had to kill those men in front of you. I didn't mean to upset you."

"I understand why you had to do it," she replied and tried to wipe the image from her mind.

"During the eight years I've been stranded here, more than twenty men died," he informed her without prompting. "We were dealing with two serial killers who attacked and killed the others for the sheer joy of it. In order to survive, we implemented our own justice system." He raised his brows while staring at her even though she didn't look at him. "Zero tolerance. We've been murder-free for nearly three years. A couple of us police the prison and keep the violence down." He chuckled. "In case you hadn't guessed, I'm public enemy number one. A split second, one moment of hesitation, and I assure you I'd be the one dead."

"I understand."

She did understand, but she'd never imagined a world so violent before. Then again, she'd never met such violent men before either.

"Do you? You haven't looked at me since I sat down," he remarked and seemed tense while straightening. "Makes me think you're either mad or afraid of me."

Alex fidgeted and still refused to look at him. She drew a deep breath and held it a moment. "I, uh, sort of saw you naked."

Damon stared at her profile with surprise then chuckled. "Think you'll be emotionally scarred for life?" he teased.

She managed a tiny laugh. "Could be."

"I suppose it's safe to assume that was a first for you," he remarked while staring at the ocean where he sat alongside her. "Well, if it doesn't bother me, it shouldn't bother you." He then considered the comment and made a face. "Of course, a good day for me is any day I don't see a naked man."

"Could be why you don't spend a lot of time at the prison," she teased while casting a glance at him.

He sighed deeply and frowned. "Too many years in the Navy and now here," he replied while reflecting back. "I'd rather be out on my own. There are thirty men in the prison, and I only like two. One is my old Navy buddy."

She finally felt comfortable enough to look at him. "What did you do to earn your place here?"

Damon eyed her, a little surprised by the blunt question.

Alex immediately fidgeted. "Sorry. I suppose that was a bit personal."

"No, you should want to know if I'm a murderer or rapist," he insisted, defending her question. He straightened proudly. "I don't tolerate rapists or child molesters. I'd love to say I'm not a murderer, but as you saw today, that's subjective. Bundy and I were Navy SEALs. That's why we took charge of policing the prison. How we got our ticket here is a totally different story." He leaned back on his hands and stretched his legs out in front of him. "We hitched a ride on the prison transport in a less than fully sanctioned rescue mission to break out our SEAL friend. After the shit hit the fan, we retained our cover as prisoners to avoid being targeted by the others."

She stared at him with a cleverly raised brow and a 'be for real' look. "Do you honestly think I'm that naive?" Alex demanded.

"Believe what you want," he casually replied. "The Navy has us MIA. They could vouch for me, although I doubt we'll ever see a rescue."

She considered his story, uncertain if she believed him or not, although something else bugged her regarding the prison. "What did happen at the prison?"

"I couldn't say. We arrived late to the party," he informed her. "When we arrived on the prison transport ship, no one from the prison greeted us. The guards from the ship went to investigate and never came back." He sank into thought a moment as if reliving that day. He shook his head. "When we finally managed to free ourselves, we found nothing but blood within the prison. No bodies. Not even the guards from our ship. Everyone had just vanished." He sighed softly. "In the eight years we've been stranded here, nothing strange has ever happened. The only reasonable explanation is someone attacked the prison, thought they'd killed everyone, and left by boat long before we managed to free ourselves from the prison transport ship. In those eight years, I've been all over this island, and I never found anything unusual."

She stared at him with surprise and mild horror. "Talk about creepy."

"Enough about the prison I call home," he announced and eyed her while grinning. "I was impressed by how you handled yourself back there today. I thought you were just *attempting* to intimidate them. I had no idea you *were* intimidating."

"Holt taught me, although it's completely different fighting for real than when we spar for fun," she informed him. "I can honestly say I prefer play fighting with Holt over the real thing."

"I'm trained in combat fighting and special ops but only limited martial arts," he informed her then chuckled. "I'm not so sure I could beat you in a fair fight."

"I'd be willing to let you win one out of three," she teased with a smile meant to mock him.

Damon raised his brows while hiding his grin. "Is that a challenge?"

Alex frowned and reconsidered. "If Holt knew, he'd be upset with me."

Damon grinned deviously. "Come on, show me what you've got, little girl."

She glared at him with a moderately offended look. "Little girl?"

"Navy trash talk," he teased then winked at her. "I'm baiting you."

She laughed at the comment. "Okay," she finally agreed. "Poles or hand-to-hand?"

"I've seen you use that pole," he announced while chuckling. "I'd like to maintain a little bit of my ego. Hand-to-hand. No hard hits." He then pointed a warning finger at her. "And no groin shots."

"I won't pull anything I wouldn't do with Holt," she insisted with an innocent smile.

Both stood and brushed the sand from their legs. Damon removed his shoes, faced her, and attempted to hide his boyish grin. He seemed a little too eager to spar with her. Alex bowed to him. Damon appeared humored and bowed in response. She took a defensive fighting stance. Damon took a military combat stance. Alex maintained no expression despite Damon's grin. Monster now moved to his belly, hung his head over the rock, and watched with apparent interest. Damon made the first move on Alex. She blocked a punch, flipped into a pinwheel using no hands and kicked him in the chest while nearly upside down. As Damon was thrown onto his backside, Alex gracefully straightened.

"One--zero," Alex announced.

Damon stared at her towering above him with surprise then picked himself up and brushed off the sand. "What the hell was that?"

She grinned. "I'm bendy."

Both again bowed and took their attack positions. Damon again moved to attack her. Alex spun into a high, roundhouse kick. Damon pulled his head back with little

126

room to spare, barely avoiding her kick. As Alex landed, he moved. She kicked the opposite direction and knocked him sideways onto the sand. Damon again picked himself up.

"So much for my ego," he muttered.

"Would you like to call no kicks above the waist?" she asked with a curious look.

"Yeah, let's try that."

They again bowed and took their fighting stances. Damon lunged for Alex. She dove to the sand and swept his legs out from under him. She was back on her feet and in position before he even landed.

Damon groaned and slowly moved to his feet. "You're like part cat or something," he remarked. "Maybe you could come at me for a change."

"Holt likes me to fight defensively only," she informed him. "I don't usually initiate."

"Fair enough," he replied. "Let's implement a 'no kicks' policy."

She conceded. They bowed and resumed their attack positions. Damon again went after Alex, throwing a punch. She blocked his soft punch with her arms and one with her leg.

"That was a kick," he was quick to point out.

"No, that was a block," she firmly insisted. "It's legal."

They resumed fighting, finally allowing Damon a few shots. Alex blocked everything he brought at her then jabbed him in the ribs and flipped him over her hip. He landed roughly in the sand. Damon lay on the sand a moment, groaned in disgust, and finally got up. He glared at her as he brushed sand from his pants.

"You're ruthless."

"And you're down four--zero."

They went into another round of blocks and punches. Alex continued to block his aggressive advances. She appeared to contemplate a kick, backed off, and left herself open to be caught. Damon immobilized her arm and finally thought he had the advantage over her. Alex tossed herself over his hip, took him off balance, and threw him to the ground while skillfully landing on top of him. Damon stared at Alex with surprise at her position over him. She straddled his hips while pinning his shoulders to the sand and grinned at him.

"Game, set, match."

Damon appeared stunned then grinned with apparent humor. "You beat me. I win."

As she hovered over him, she stared at him with surprise by the comment. "How do you figure that?" she demanded.

Damon flipped her onto her back and pinned her to the sand with his body in a compromising position. Alex stared with surprise at Damon now on top of her.

"It's subjective," he teased then kissed her quickly but passionately on the mouth. He taunted her with a lustful smile and jumped to his feet.

Alex immediately stood and faced him, feeling more baffled than upset. She didn't even know what had just happened or why he was so pleased with himself.

"I've enjoyed being repeatedly thrown to the ground, but I should probably quit while I'm ahead," he teased then approached his pack and slipped into his shoes.

Alex watched him with some bewilderment. "You confuse me. I'm obviously missing something," she announced while continuing to stare at him. "Why are you suddenly in a hurry? Don't make me ask Holt to explain it to me."

He stared at her with an oddly concerned look. "You're not going to tell Holt, are you?" Damon immediately frowned. "He doesn't approve of us talking let alone rolling around the sand together."

It then dawned on her what had happened, and she groaned with realization. "Oh, damn it," she cried out then shook her head. "I did it again, didn't I?"

"Now I'm confused," Damon remarked while staring at her with a baffled look as he cocked his head. "Did what again?"

"Holt specifically told me not to straddle any part of a man's body," she remarked then frowned, annoyed with herself. "I wasn't thinking."

Damon stared at her with his mouth hanging open and appeared surprised while considering her comment. "He said what?"

"It affects brain activity and causes sexual responses," she replied and shook her head shamefully. "I'm sorry if what I did bothered you."

Damon stared at her with a loss for words. He finally shook his head and raised his brows demandingly. "I recommend you don't take sexual advice from Holt." He set his pack down, took her hand in his, and looked into her eyes. "You have my permission to straddle any part of my body you want." A grin crossed his face. "I enjoy sexual responses with great enthusiasm. It reminds me that I'm still alive."

Damon smiled warmly and kissed the back of her hand. As his lips touched her hand, Alex could only stare helplessly. Her heart was pounding, although she was uncertain why. The strange ache throughout her body was even more troubling. He stared into her eyes a moment longer then gently touched her face and brushed his lips past hers. Alex tensed while her heart pounded in her chest. Damon kissed her warmly but passionately while pulling her against him. She liked the way his body felt against hers, and there was no denying she enjoyed his mouth pressing against hers.

Alex nervously returned the kiss, although she was uncertain if she did it correctly. Damon kissed her more passionately and with some aggression. She assumed she'd done it correctly, judging by his response. The sensation was unlike anything she'd ever experienced before. Her pounding heart and the strange ache throughout her body seemed to increase to the point where it was almost painful. Alex returned the passionate kiss, hoping the feeling wouldn't end. Damon broke off the kiss and groaned.

"I need to go before I make a very bad decision," he informed her timidly then hesitated while staring into her eyes. Alex hadn't moved, remaining happily clueless. "Ah, hell, he can kill me if he wants to."

Damon pulled her against him and kissed her with passion and aggression. Alex immediately returned the kiss with more enthusiasm now that his body was again pressed against hers. As his hands traveled her body, she felt an overwhelming desire. She was suddenly curious about sex and wondered if that's where they were heading. Damon again broke off the kiss and appeared almost frustrated, although he refused to release her. She was glad because his body felt good against hers

"Stop encouraging my bad behavior," he insisted as his hands continued to travel her body, almost as if he could no longer control them.

She stared into his eyes, uncertain how she was supposed to respond. "I never really had a boyfriend," she gently informed him. "I like the way you feel against me." She hesitated and stared at him with concern. "Is that wrong?"

For a moment, Damon stared at her as if unable to respond. "No, of course not," he insisted while practically fumbling over his words. "I just don't want to take advantage of you. Your innocence is a bit intimidating." Damon finally released her and took her hand without taking his eyes from hers. "I'll be at the hot springs tomorrow afternoon. If we see each other, Holt can't know. He'll never allow it."

"If I agree to meet you there, can we take it slow?" she asked.

"I'll gladly let you set the pace," he replied warmly while caressing her hand in his. "I'm just happy to hold you."

Chapter Thirty

Later that afternoon, Alex and Holt sat at the cabin table with cups of tea before them. Alex was preoccupied with what happened on the beach with Damon. The entire incident was confusing, since she didn't understand her emotions, and she certainly couldn't ask Holt to help her better understand them either. She wasn't sure how long she stared into her tea before Holt became concerned by her silence.

"Are you okay, dear?" he finally asked. "Did you want to talk about what happened today?"

Alex looked at him with surprise by the question and nearly choked. "What?"

"The incident at the pond," he replied while fidgeting. "It's obvious it's still bothering you."

She couldn't help but think what a sweet man he was, but she couldn't tell him the truth. "No, I'm okay with that," she replied in a timid tone.

"Did you talk to Damon before he left?" Holt asked with some apprehension.

Alex felt her heart pound at the question, but she couldn't let Holt sense anything had happened between Damon and her.

"He stopped by the beach," she announced and only briefly glanced at him. "I know you want me to stay away from him, but I thought it would be rude to avoid him."

"I know you don't like or understand it, Alex, but it's for your own good."

"We're bound to run into each other with you trading goods," she practically insisted. "Maybe you should get to know him, so I don't have to avoid him."

Holt rolled his eyes and groaned, obviously not wanting to have that conversation with her. "He's a prisoner. What more do I need to know?" he remarked with irritation then seemed to tense. "Eventually he won't seem so bad, he'll get you pregnant, and I'll be wondering how the hell I let it happen."

Alex stared at him with disbelief at the comment and cleverly raised her brows. "There has to be a lot of gaps filled in before I end up pregnant."

"You have no options," Holt insisted while staring into her eyes with a strange seriousness as if he were reading her mind. "Believe me. Eventually, he's going to look good to you."

Although she was wondering how he seemed to know what she was thinking, she hid her feelings.

"You're worrying about something that is probably irrelevant, but since you brought it up," she boldly announced then shifted uncomfortably. "The thought of never having a physical relationship does kind of bother me a little."

He seemed to tense, drew a deep breath, and smiled sympathetically. "It's perfectly natural for you to feel that way," he informed her.

Holt approached the pantry and returned with a bottle. He poured each of them a glass of moonshine and placed one in front of her.

"Sorry, I need to be buzzed to have this conversation," he remarked.

Alex sipped the contents and immediately made a face. "Oh, that's foul," she gasped with horror and set the cup down. Her eyes then met his with seriousness. "I'm not asking you to fulfill that role, Holt."

"You think Damon might though, huh?" he remarked while raising his brows.

Again, his mind-reading abilities were starting to frighten her. She resisted responding to the question for fear of any recourse.

"I'm sure he'd be willing to violate your body, but I doubt he'd provide the sort of intimacy you're looking for," Holt insisted as he took another large swallow of the disgusting substance. "And when you finally realize that, he'll be impossible to ditch. I understand how you feel, but would it really be worth it?"

"Exactly why you should get to know him," she again insisted. "You'd be able to figure out what sort of man he is. You understand the inner workings of men."

"Yes, you're right. I do understand the inner workings of men. Damon hasn't seen a woman in eight years," Holt announced sternly. "He's going to do or say whatever it takes to get you to have sex with him."

"I realize I run the risk of disappointment, but I'll never know if I don't ever take the chance," she informed him.

Holt groaned and took another large swallow of moonshine from the glass. He shook his head in disgust. "You're not prepared to deal with a man like Damon," he insisted without hesitation. "I don't want to see you get hurt."

"I also don't want to die an old virgin," she boldly countered.

Holt tensed at the comment, finished his drink, and choked on the foul substance. "God, it tastes like kerosene," he gasped then met her gaze. "Not exactly a role I'm interested in fulfilling." He then considered their situation. "Perhaps if we shared the bottom bunk, you'd find the closeness you're looking for without the need for a sexual relationship."

She felt her heart sink. "One's not really a substitute for the other."

"Please, Alex, it's all I have to offer."

She stared at him and didn't know how she could openly refuse to at least attempt his suggestion. She loved him dearly, but it wasn't a need for intimacy she craved. Honestly, it was Damon's body against hers.

"Okay," she announced with a sigh, reluctantly giving in. "We'll try it your way."

Chapter Thirty-one

Alex woke early the following morning after having slept in the bottom bunk with Holt. Holt clung to her from behind while presumably asleep. Monster's tail and front legs hung down from the upper bunk. At least someone was benefiting from Holt's ridiculous idea. Alex remained deep in thought. Holt seemed to wake, sighed softly, and rolled onto his back. Alex turned on the bed to face Holt, who stared at Monster's tail hanging from the upper bunk.

"Sleep well?" she chirped with enthusiasm, already knowing the answer.

She had felt him tossing and turning most of the night. Obviously, it had to do with her.

"Not particularly."

"Anything to do with my sleeping next to you?" she asked slyly while hiding her smile.

"Don't be silly," he announced with little reaction then frowned while scratching his brow. "It had everything to do with you sleeping next to me."

Alex moved against Holt, clung to him, and placed her head on his shoulder.

He held her while remaining weary and frustrated. "My comfort isn't important," he informed her. "I'm doing this for you."

"I know the sort of sacrifice you're willing to make, but I'm rejecting the idea," she informed him and lifted her head to meet his gaze. "If you really care about my happiness, you'll get to know Damon."

Holt released her, quickly sat up, and stared into her eyes with alarm. "Did something happen that I should know about?" he suddenly gasped as his eyes widened. "Did he ask you to have sex with him?"

"No, of course not," she insisted, although she was quite sure she was the aggressor in what did happen. "He's very respectful."

"Men can be charming while taking advantage of young women," Holt informed her. "They'll say and do anything to get a woman to have sex with them." He frowned at the thought. "Even I was guilty of being excessively charming when I was younger."

"Ironic," she announced. "Why is it everyone else is entitled to make mistakes except me? If we'd never been stranded on this island, I'm sure I would have dated by now, and there's a good chance I'd have slept with at least one guy too. Why am I being punished for mistakes I haven't even made yet?"

Holt groaned and held his head. "Can we talk about this later?" he asked while moaning. "It's too early in the morning to be drinking moonshine."

"Of course we can discuss it later," she announced while springing up from the bunk then glared at him. "As long as we actually discuss it."

"You have my word, Alex," he replied.

That was good enough for her. Holt always kept his word.

Chapter Thirty-two

Alex entered the clearing to the hot springs with her pole clutched firmly in her hand. Monster could be heard following her from within the trees. There was no sign of Damon, for which she was almost grateful. She was so anxious; her heart nearly pounded through her chest. She didn't like lying to Holt, but she also knew she had to meet Damon. She had to understand what she was feeling and deal with those emotions. Alex attempted to relax and sat on a large rock.

A mammoth, meaty spider dropped onto the rock near her. It was such a weighty creature; she actually heard it thump as it landed near her. Alex cried out and sprang to her feet. She didn't fear snakes much anymore, now that she understood the creatures, but those hairy spiders still gave her a serious case of the heebie-jeebies. Monster pounced onto the rock and snapped up the meaty spider.

The spider partially wriggled from Monster's mouth before he crunched it between his teeth and feasted on its hairy body. Alex felt her stomach turn and made a face at the sound.

"Oh, that is so disgusting."

Monster suddenly crouched and growled while staring at something.

"You could have left him at home," Damon announced from nearby.

Alex turned and saw Damon entering the clearing from the path.

Damon smiled almost timidly and seemed somewhat tense. "I was sure you wouldn't show."

"I had a long talk with Holt," she informed him proudly. "He promised to get to know you and give me his honest opinion."

He chuckled while grinning. "It's been a while since I had to impress a girl's father," he teased. "I'd better start working on my charm." He eyed her pole and held back his laugh. "How about we call a truce and disarm for our first date?"

Alex set her pole aside as Damon removed his machete and placed it near her pole. He opened his pack and removed a blanket and mangoes.

"The store was all out of wine," he teased then removed a flower and smiled charmingly. "But I did get you this."

Alex eyed the flower while smiling at the thought. "That's poisonous," she casually informed him. "You'll want to wash your hands."

Damon frowned and tossed the flower over his shoulder. "Figures." He washed his hands with the bottled water then wiped them on his pants. "Care to soak in the hot tub before we dine?"

She eyed him suspiciously then smiled. "As long as you don't expect me to skinny dip."

"Undergarments are permitted but not required," he informed her. "I'm not fond of wet underwear. I'm going commando."

"I'll be sure to turn my head this time."

"Suit yourself."

Alex avoided watching as Damon removed his clothes and entered the hot spring. She stripped down to her underwear and bra with some insecurity while Damon waded within the hot spring watching her.

"The women's clothes I'd sent fit nicely," he announced.

Alex cast a look then joined him in the hot spring. "Why were there women's clothes in a man's prison?" she asked while remaining a safe distance from him once in the water.

"There must have been a nurse," he informed her. "There were nursing uniforms." He hesitated then smiled. "Now that you know about the prison, I could bring them to you." He then indicated the back edge of the hot springs he occupied. "There's a little ledge over here to sit on. You'd be more comfortable."

She eyed him suspiciously. "I'm debating how close I should get to a naked man."

"Six inches minimum safe distance," he teased.

Alex eyed him, not understanding the joke. He laughed at her expense. She uncertainly moved alongside him.

"So, do you come here a lot?" she asked.

"Is that your best pick-up line?" he teased.

"Monster and I come every week, but he doesn't like the hot water," she informed him.

"Does he swim?"

"He's an amazing swimmer," she admitted. "He bodysurfs in the ocean. I think he must be part reptile or something."

"I'm surprised Holt hasn't attempted to dissect him," Damon muttered.

"Please don't give him any ideas," she announced in a tone that was almost serious. "We found him in the stream, but he probably fell in somewhere from the south side of the island."

"I've never seen anything like him around here during my tour of duty," he informed her.

"I assure you, he didn't want you to see him," she remarked, "but if there had been others, Monster would have found them."

"I'm grateful he's one of a kind," Damon announced while eying the large creature where he relaxed on a rock near the hot spring. "He's a bit intimidating."

"He's a pussycat," she insisted. "He'd never harm a fly." She then considered the comment. "Although, he doesn't mind eating the occasional spider."

Once they'd concluded their conversation about Monster, there was an awkward silence. Alex felt the need to speak what was on her mind and get it out into the open.

"Holt thinks you're just after sex," she finally blurted out.

Damon was slightly surprised by her blunt honesty. "Men want sex; it's a proven fact, but it's not all we want; he knows that," Damon informed her. "When you live without female companionship for eight years, you miss more than just the sex. Personally, I miss the intimacy that goes along with it."

"I think that's what I'm looking for."

He chuckled while eying her. "Nothing says intimacy more than sitting on a naked man's lap," he informed her. "Although you may get more of an education than you expected."

Alex moved onto Damon's lap, surprising him, and nervously placed her arms around his neck. She tensed and appeared embarrassed while staring into his eyes as he held her.

"You weren't kidding, huh?"

"I wasn't actually expecting you to take me up on that," he announced then gently cleared his throat. "I could have given you fair warning."

"Am I making you uncomfortable?" she asked with concern.

"No," he announced while groaning. "Quite the opposite."

They stared into each other's eyes only a moment before Damon lowered his mouth to hers and kissed her warmly but passionately. Alex immediately returned the kiss with a little more enthusiasm and allowed her hand to run gently along his chest. Damon's hand moved along her thigh beneath the water but resisted making any bold moves. He gently broke off the kiss then warmly kissed her neck and throat as his hand traveled her back while his other hand aggressively caressed her leg.

Damon groaned and resumed kissing her mouth with more aggression. Alex returned the aggressive kiss while repositioning herself on his lap and straddled his legs so she was facing him. Damon appeared surprised, gasped softly, but quickly returned to kissing her while moaning. He pulled her hips closer to his, melding her lightly clothed body against his naked one. Alex gasped and tensed by the sensation of him pressing against her. Damon immediately broke off the kiss and appeared embarrassed.

"I'm sorry. I thought--" He hid his smile and shook his head. "Never mind. I'll behave."

Alex had a difficult time keeping her hands from caressing his bare shoulders and chest while her body was mostly pressed against his. Her heart was pounding, and her body was aching.

"No, it's okay," she gasped.

He didn't require much encouragement. Damon groaned and resumed kissing her with renewed passion. Alex continued to caress his bare chest and shoulders while enjoying the sensation of his arousal pressed against her underwear beneath the hot water. A moment passed, and

Damon again pulled her hips against him. She gasped with surprise and broke off the kiss.

"I'm sorry," Damon announced and loosened his grip on her waist and buttocks. "My brain shut down the moment you put your legs around me. You should probably rethink that position."

Alex stared into his eyes a moment then moved off him. She tossed her panties onto the rocks behind him and her bra quickly followed. Damon appeared stunned by her actions. Alex moved back on top of him, straddled his legs, and again clung to him. As they kissed wildly, she could feel him pressed against her. Damon slowly pulled her against him. Alex gasped and stopped kissing him. She clung to him and shut her eyes. Damon seemed hesitant then kissed her neck and throat while gently pulling her hips against him. She let out a slight cry as Damon groaned lowly. He buried his head into her neck and again pulled her hips against him. Alex gasped as Damon groaned more loudly.

"Are you okay?" he whispered in her ear.

Alex nodded while breathing heavily. "Just don't stop," she whispered.

Damon kissed her warmly and with less aggression while pulling her against him. Alex relaxed and returned the warm kiss. She broke off the kiss and clung to him as he gently made love to her. A little while later, Damon held Alex against him. Both nuzzled the other's necks while breathing heavily.

"I didn't intend for that to happen," he gently informed her while hiding his smile. "Of course, now that we've set that precedence, it's going to be expected whenever we see each other."

She pulled back and eyed him with a curious look. "Says who?"

Damon smiled deviously. "Says me."

She attempted to relax but remained tense. "Holt's worried I'll get pregnant."

His expression suddenly dropped as if he hadn't even thought about the possibility. "Oh," he muttered with some concern. "Had I actually been thinking, I would have considered that."

"Well, now you have something to discuss with Holt," she announced while smiling as she patted his chest. "He can tell you what time of month to keep your hands off me."

"Unfortunately, he'll kill me just for asking."

Chapter Thirty-three

After their erotic afternoon picnic, Damon and Alex walked through the woods while holding hands and talking. Both could barely control their childlike grins. Damon stopped near the stream and turned to face her.

"I think this is where we part company," he informed her while attempting a frown, but his boyish smile still beamed through. "I'm in too good a mood to have Holt kill me."

"I wish you didn't have to go back to the prison," she pouted, allowing her good mood to fade away at the thought of him leaving again. "I wish you could stay with me."

"That's a real temptation. You or thirty despicable men--and Bundy. You definitely win that one," he announced while grinning his approval. "I just don't think

Holt will be nearly as enthusiastic about us shacking up with him. But, if Holt ever warms up to the idea, we could always convert the upper floor into a place of our own, and Bundy could live downstairs with Holt."

"Who gets Monster?"

"I'll have to think about that one." Damon pulled Alex into his arms and held her against him while nuzzling her. "How about we meet tomorrow on the west beach? Say late morning? I'll bring a deck of cards and teach you poker."

"Stud or draw?"

Damon frowned and reconsidered the comment. "Maybe I'll bring the chessboard instead."

He kissed her long and passionately then smiled and headed toward the nearby path. Alex turned and headed for the lighthouse, although her mind was still back at the hot spring, reliving their passionate lovemaking in the water and then the follow-up session on the blanket. She paused and looked back; wanting one more peek at her newly acquired boyfriend. Damon had turned as well and watched her. They exchanged lustful smiles and continued on their separate ways.

§

Alex entered the lighthouse clearing and paused a moment to stare at the cabin, which somehow seemed different now. Monster scurried up the side of the lighthouse, but Alex was reluctant to enter and face Holt after her afternoon of unbridled passion with the forbidden outsider. While she attempted to psych herself to face Holt, he walked out of the cabin, saw her, and smiled in his usual cheerful manner.

"Have fun today?" he asked.

Alex felt her heart skip a beat while her thoughts strayed to her erotic afternoon and how disappointed Holt would be if he found out. She forced a smile and attempted to act as if nothing had happened, although it wasn't easy.

"Oh, yes," she announced while attempting to keep from sounding too cheerful. "A spider tried to abduct me, but Monster saved the day." She then made a face. "And ate it."

"Keeping the island safe one spider at a time," he teased while grinning. "And will you be meeting Damon tomorrow as well?"

Alex stared at him with shock. Her heart nearly pounded from her chest, but she couldn't seem to control it. "What makes you think I saw him today?"

"I spotted his tracks in the woods earlier," he informed her. "Out of respect for you, I didn't get close enough to spy. Judging by the sounds I was hearing, I suspect I would have been rather upset by what I may have seen."

Alex felt her heart sink and didn't know what to say to Holt. "I'm sorry I lied to you, Holt."

Holt smirked and raised his brows. "I'm pretty sure you're not," he remarked then shook his head. "I'm just looking out for you, Alex. I know why you felt you had to lie. I won't stand in the way, but if anything happens, be honest with me. I just want to protect you."

She thought for sure he'd tear into her about lying and for having sex with the man he specifically asked her to avoid for her own welfare.

"No more lies, I promise," she replied gently.

Holt inhaled deeply and managed a smile. "Good," he announced a little more cheerfully. "Now let's go inside and discuss your birth control options."

As he turned and headed inside, Alex lowered her head and groaned. She followed him into the cabin, reluctant to have that uncomfortable conversation.

§

Damon walked along the bland prison corridor and headed for the cellblock he called home. Everything seemed unusually quiet for early evening. There was a faint clunk echoing from somewhere within the prison, although its origin would be difficult to detect. A man was heard crying out. Damon tossed his pack down, removed his machete and hurried back along the corridor toward the kitchen area. The male cries turned into bloodcurdling screams. Damon picked up his pace and ran along the corridor as the screams became louder. He ran around the corner and suddenly slid to the floor. His machete flew from his hand.

Damon was momentarily dazed and attempted to sit up as the screaming stopped. He looked to his right where his machete had fallen and saw a large streak of fresh blood. He soon realized he had slipped in a pool of blood. Damon grabbed his machete, sprang to his feet, and followed the blood to a man lying on the corridor floor. His throat was torn out, and he appeared to be gutted. Apart from the body, there was no one else in the corridor. He heard another scream coming from deeper within the prison walls.

"Bundy?" Damon gasped.

Chapter Thirty-four

Alex slept peacefully in her bunk while Holt tossed and turned on the lower bunk. Alex woke, sensing Holt's restlessness. When she opened her eyes, she saw Monster hanging from the ceiling above her bunk with his face directly in front of hers. Alex jumped and kept from screaming. Monster wailed softly, indicating something was wrong. As Alex sat up, Monster leaped from the ceiling and onto the floor, causing the entire floor to vibrate. He wildly scratched at the door, leaving deep grooves in the wood. Since he was able to leave the lighthouse through the open upstairs window, it was unusual for him to be at the door. Alex and Holt jumped from their bunks, startled by the noise and his actions.

"What's going on?" Holt gasped.

"I don't know," Alex cried out with alarm. "Something has Monster upset."

Alex opened the door and watched Monster run from the lighthouse cabin. Holt tossed her a pole, grabbed his own, and they hurried after him. Once outside, Alex and Holt spotted Monster on the path leading into the woods. They hurried along the dark path following Monster.

"What's gotten into him?" Holt demanded.

"I don't know," she announced with concern, "but it's not like him to stay on the ground. He definitely wants us to follow him."

Monster stopped and nudged something on the path. Both slowed. Holt approached cautiously. Alex raised her pole defensively and followed. As they got closer, they saw Damon sprawled on the ground badly beaten and bleeding. Alex cried out and hurried to his side. Holt took a defensive stance and looked around the dark woods with his pole raised as if expecting someone to leap out and attack them.

"He's alive, but he's been hurt badly," she announced while casting a quick glance at Holt.

Holt still wasn't convinced they were safe from whatever attacked Damon and remained on high alert. "Let's get him back to the lighthouse," he remarked. "I don't like being exposed out here. We don't know who attacked him and if he's still out there."

Damon remained unconscious on the bottom bunk.

His shirt had been removed revealing scratches across his chest, strange marks on his arms, and bruises on his body. Holt cleaned the scratches while Alex applied pressure with a cloth to his bleeding temple. She cast several looks at Holt.

"Will he be okay?" she asked with concern.

"Nothing appears to be broken," Holt informed her while tending to his first aid. "I'm guessing he made it quite a distance before collapsing, possibly from exhaustion." He straightened on the edge of the bunk and observed the unconscious man. "I don't think any of his injuries are life-threatening."

"Why won't he wake up?"

"Give him time, Alex," Holt announced while casting a glance at her. "It's possible he has a concussion. He'll wake up when he's ready."

An hour had passed, and Damon still remained unconscious. Alex sat on the bed alongside the injured man while Holt made tea. Damon slowly woke and groaned. Monster peered down from the top bunk, studied the injured man, and gurgled softly. Alex gently touched Damon's face.

"Hey, can you hear me?" she whispered.

Damon stared at her with disorientation. "What happened?"

"Don't you remember?"

He appeared confused then looked at Monster staring down at him from the top bunk. Damon suddenly sat up with alarm.

"It was Monster," he cried out in panic. "He attacked us. He tried to kill me!"

Holt approached them and stared at Damon with concern and confusion.

Alex stared as well as her mouth hung open. "Damon, Monster found you," she informed him. "He took us to you in the woods."

"He was at the prison," Damon insisted while glaring at the creature. "He attacked Bundy. I tried to stop him, and then he turned on me." He pressed his back against the bedframe while staring with fear at Monster. "I'm telling you, he scratched and bit me! He killed one of the other men!"

Alex and Holt exchanged puzzled looks then returned their attention to the fearful man.

"We were on the beach until dark," Alex informed him. "He had dinner with us and spent the rest of the evening chasing rats around the lighthouse. He never left. He couldn't have been at the prison."

Holt's eyes suddenly widened with concern. "Monster was washed downstream from the south side of the island," he announced. "There could be another."

"But that was six years ago," Alex protested. "Surely, they would have seen one during that time."

"Monster is reptilian. Reptiles come from eggs," Holt informed her. "He could have hatched and been washed downstream to us. The eggs could lie dormant for years. Something may have caused another egg to hatch." He raised his brows while staring at her. "It only took a few months for Monster to grow full size."

"I know every inch of that prison," Damon insisted. "I never found any eggs."

"Just because you didn't see them, that doesn't mean they weren't there," Holt insisted. "Some reptiles bury their eggs. When the right environment stimulates the egg, they hatch."

Damon straightened and attempted to climb from the bed. "I have to go back," he announced. "I have to make sure Bundy is okay."

"You're in no condition to go anywhere tonight," Holt insisted. "You need to rest." He stared at him a moment and appeared curious. "Why did you come here? You would have been safer in the prison."

"When the creature took off, I was afraid he was coming back to kill you and Alex. I needed to stop him," Damon informed them. "If it wasn't Monster, it could still be in the prison. Bundy's in danger. We don't leave our men behind."

153

"You'll be no good to him injured and exhausted. Running through the jungle in the dark with a vicious creature on the loose is just plain foolish," Holt remarked sternly. "When it's light, Monster and I will accompany you back to the prison. He'll be able to alert us to any creatures lurking around."

"You're not going without me," Alex protested.

"You're not going into that prison, Alex," Holt snarled.

"I go where you go," she retorted. "If something happens to you, I'm not doing this alone."

Damon was just as concerned as Holt was for her safety. "You stay outside the fence. I mean it," Damon stated firmly. "I don't want those horny bastards knowing you exist."

Holt muttered, "Look who's talking."

Damon glared at Holt.

Chapter Thirty-five

The following morning, Holt, Damon, and Alex approached the overgrown fence surrounding the prison. Holt and Alex carried their poles for weapons as they approached the opening several yards away. Monster could be heard jumping around within the trees. They stopped several feet from the opening in the gate.

Holt turned to face Alex. "You wait out here. Make sure Monster stays with you," he insisted. "We don't want the others to see him."

Monster crawled down the tree headfirst. He had a Chinese warrior symbol painted on his forehead in bright yellow. It was Alex's idea to mark him, so he wouldn't be accidentally mistaken for a hostile creature, in the event there was another like him lurking about the prison.

"I will," she announced. "I certainly don't want him accidentally killed either."

"Well, he'll be hard to miss, that's for sure," Holt replied and eyed the symbol on the creature's forehead. "If there's any trouble, I want you to go back to the lighthouse."

Alex nodded in response. As Holt hugged her, she returned the long embrace with her own concerns.

"You intend to come back, don't you?" she whispered as he held her.

"Yes, of course," he replied and released her.

Alex appeared unconvinced as Holt turned and walked away. Damon approached and kissed her warmly then held her face in his hands.

"I want you to know if anything happens to me," he announced delicately, "don't date other men."

Alex smiled and playfully slapped his shoulder. As Damon approached Holt, Holt glared at him.

Damon glared back. "What?"

The men entered through the opening in the gate and disappeared into the prison grounds. Alex looked at Monster and gave him a slight nod. Monster backed up the tree in reverse almost as fast as he had moved forward. Alex jumped into the tree after him. They climbed high enough to see over the gate. For the first time, Alex was able to view the large, stone prison complete with guard towers surrounded in overgrown fences. Despite its age and neglect, the building was sound and solid with no noticeable breaches or broken windows.

The fence had some breaches, particularly among the barbed wire covering the top. The wildly growing jungle vegetation was more than the barbed wire could handle. Most of the yard was overgrown with vegetation as well. There was little reason or ambition among the prisoners to maintain the large yard. Despite the condition of most of the grounds, a large portion appeared to be a well-cared for garden. She could see Holt and Damon heading toward the building. No one greeted them, which made Alex nervous. Alex looked at Monster on the branch above her.

"I wonder if it's always so quiet this early in the morning," she remarked.

Monster watched Damon and Holt in the distance, not taking his eyes off them until they disappeared into the building. He gurgled a soft response but remained focused on the prison. Monster suddenly sniffed the air and appeared excited. Alex looked around at his oddly alert state. His reaction was unusual, considering he didn't give her the usual warning sign.

"What is it?" she asked and continued to scan the area. "Is something wrong?"

Monster leaped to another tree with speed and agility. Alex climbed down the tree, landed on her feet, and took off through the woods after the swiftly traveling creature, following the sounds of rustling trees above her.

"Monster! Get back here!"

Alex reached a clearing several yards away. She listened to the rustling within the tree while attempting to locate him.

"Monster?"

A large black mass fell roughly to the ground with a loud thud, startling Alex. At first, she didn't understand how he'd fallen from the tree without a branch breaking. She then realized Monster rolled around in a tight ball with another creature exactly like him. They leaped apart, took defensive fighting stances, and wildly swished their tails while hissing at each other. Their teeth were bared as they slowly circled the other. Alex clutched her pole and stared at the scene in horror. Holt had been right. She wouldn't have believed it if she hadn't seen it for herself.

Monster leaped for the other creature, tackling it to the ground. They rolled around violently while biting and slashing at each other with claws and their tails. Monster ended up on top of the other creature from behind while clinging to it and bit it on the back of its neck. Alex stared a moment with concern then uncertainly straightened as her expression dropped.

"Okay, that's *not* fighting."

Alex grimaced and turned her head as Monster mated with the female creature. She could hear their loud wails as Monster humped the female. After several minutes, Alex eyed the mating pair and frowned, wishing they'd wrap things up a little faster. Monster finally leaped away from the female, who immediately turned and hissed at him as if displeased with their romp. Monster playfully bounced around then tossed himself to the ground and rolled around, displaying his enthusiasm.

"Okay, you got laid," Alex grumbled with disapproval. "Enough celebrating. How do we stop your new girlfriend from trying to kill people?"

Without warning, the female creature leaped on top of Monster's back and bit him on the base of the neck. Monster violently rolled, taking the female with him. This time, the sounds weren't that of play or mating. The new frightening sounds were vicious. Monster slashed at the female with his tail, preventing her from ripping out his throat. They circled each other while hissing then lunged for each other. Alex watched in fear, uncertain if Monster could stop the female from killing him.

Monster took the female down, grabbed her by the throat with his mouth, and violently tossed his head. With a hideous crack, he snapped her neck. The female creature fell limp. Monster released her throat with bloodied, exposed teeth, and growled. He leaped off her, spun toward Alex with bared, bloodstained teeth, and wildly thrashed his long tail. It cracked like a bullwhip. Alex stared at Monster, paralyzed with fear at the rage that seemed to be directed at her. Had he gotten a taste for killing? Is that all it took to turn his kind violent?

"Monster, what's gotten into you?" she gasped while clinging defensively to her pole.

Monster suddenly leaped for Alex ten feet away from him. Alex screamed and rolled with her pole into a crouched position, prepared to defend herself even though she'd never beaten Monster in their play fights. Monster collided with another creature mid-air not far from Alex's back. Both creatures fell to the ground while clawing and biting each other. Alex stared with horror. There had been more than one? They pulled apart for a brief moment and circled each other while growling and hissing.

The female creature leaped for Monster. Monster spun and whipped his tail at her, striking her harshly across the chest. The force of the hit sent her backward into a nearby tree. She struck the tree with tremendous force. The creature fell to the ground, twitched slightly, and stopped moving. Monster wailed loudly as if asserting his dominance. He suddenly turned, leaped into the nearby tree, and thumped his tail against the trunk as a warning to her. Alex climbed the tree and joined him. Monster snarled toward the prison. Alex looked from the silent prison to Monster's frozen gaze at the building.

"What is it?" she gasped while nervously looking from Monster to the prison. "Are there more inside?"

Monster snorted as his tail violently cracked against the tree leaving a deep groove with violence she'd never seen before. Alex appeared concerned while staring at Monster.

"I know you understand me, Monster, and I know you choose not to listen sometimes," she announced firmly, "but if we go in there, you have to stay with me. There are men in there who might think you're one of the bad ones and try to kill you." She drew a deep breath and held it a moment. "Look at me if you understand."

Monster looked at Alex.

Her eyes widened with realization. "I knew it. I knew you understood every word I've ever said," she proclaimed then turned serious. "We need to find Holt and Damon. I'm counting on you to track them."

He gurgled his response, which she somehow understood. Alex climbed down the tree while Monster leaped onto the nearby fence. She hurried after him as he crawled along the fence then scurried through the open gate and landed softly on the ground. Alex entered behind him with her pole securely in hand.

Chapter Thirty-six

Alex and Monster finally reached the building and approached the open, steel door leading into the security area just before the general population areas. The prison was little more than bland, painted concrete walls, floors, and ceilings with metal bars strategically placed throughout. Dismal and uninspiring were the perfect words to describe the prison interior. Monster sniffed the air then scurried along the wall and onto the ceiling. Alex hurried after him. He stopped near an open cell door leading to one of many corridors.

The place was a maze of corridors with open cell doors everywhere. She slowly approached the opening. Monster passed through the open doorway from the ceiling. Alex cautiously followed him and entered the corridor. She stared at the massive amount of blood down the wall and on the floor. The blood streaked down the corridor and ended near a doorway as if a body was dragged. Monster scurried along the ceiling and again stopped to smell the air. He thumped his tail against the ceiling. Alex quickly moved against the wall.

Both approached the doorway with caution. She silently entered the massive kitchen. The kitchen was in desperate need of modern updates. Many of the appliances appeared rusted and not capable of functioning properly. A few areas were neat and tidy, possibly the ones mostly used, while other areas were loaded with dirty, rusted cookware, bugs, and rats. Monster remained on the ceiling and guided her through the mammoth maze of a kitchen. He suddenly stopped and stood frozen.

Alex approached while clutching her pole. There was blood on the closed steel door before her. She reached for the handle, pulled open the door, and jumped back into an attack stance. Three men jumped with alarm and stared at Alex from where they hid inside the pantry. Their looks of horror slowly turned to shock upon seeing a woman. Alex remained in attack position.

"Who are you, and where in the world did you come from?" Bundy asked.

Bundy was in excellent, physical condition. He obviously worked out regularly the same as Damon. He kept his light brown hair buzzed close to his scalp with a definite military appearance. He was ordinary looking, although not unattractive. His muscle mass was probably enough to gain plenty of female attention in the outside world. Alex didn't answer his question and remained in attack position. She didn't know these men, and she wasn't in the mood for small talk.

"Where's Damon?" she demanded.

Bundy stared at her with surprise. "You know Damon?" he gasped.

"Where is he?" she again demanded without answering his question.

The two remaining men, Tyler and Miller, stood within the pantry doorway, unable to take their eyes off the first woman they'd seen in years. Tyler and Miller were both in their late thirties to early forties and took better care of themselves than the last two men Alex had met from the prison. Although unshaven in days, Tyler had obviously bathed recently and his clothes were fairly clean. He seemed to take some pride in his overall health, keeping mostly fit. Miller was slightly overweight, but he was clean-shaven and wore clean clothes and obviously bathed regularly as well.

"We haven't seen him," Miller insisted. "We've been hiding in the pantry all night."

Bundy stepped out of the pantry and joined Alex in the kitchen. Alex reestablished her attack stance, threatening him with a look. Bundy stopped and put his hands in the air.

"You've got the wrong idea," he informed her. "We're not going to hurt you."

She'd heard that line before. She didn't fall for it last time, and she wasn't about to fall for it now.

Miller saw Monster on the ceiling. "Oh, shit!" he cried out. "There it is!"

Miller shut the pantry door, locking Bundy in the kitchen with Alex. Bundy saw Monster, cried out, and spun toward the pantry door. He attempted to open it, but it wouldn't budge.

"Hurry! Inside," Bundy cried out. "It's on the ceiling!"

"For the hard-core criminal type, you're not very brave," she snarled. "That's just Monster. He's with me. He's one of the good guys."

Bundy uncertainly turned and eyed Monster on the ceiling. Monster bared his teeth and appeared to sneer at Bundy. Bundy again screamed and attempted to open the door. Monster hissed as if laughing.

Alex eyed Monster and frowned her disapproval. "That wasn't very nice."

Bundy released the door that obviously wasn't opening, stared at the unaggressive creature on the ceiling, and then faced Alex.

"Why are you looking for Damon?"

"We don't leave our men behind," she replied. "You may want to remain hidden. Those creatures can be nasty."

Alex lowered her pole then turned to leave. Monster scurried across the ceiling toward the kitchen door.

"We don't leave our men behind?" Bundy repeated with surprise. "He told you?"

Alex turned and looked back at the man. "How he ended up here? Yes, he told me."

"I'm Bundy," he proclaimed.

She stared at him a moment with surprise then relaxed slightly. "Oh, you're the friend he came back for," she announced simply. "You should probably come with us then. He'll be happy to see you."

Bundy looked at the closed pantry door, made a face, and waved his hand. "Ah, screw them." He looked back at her and motioned her onward. "Let's go."

Alex and Bundy followed Monster from the kitchen and along the corridor. Bundy watched the large creature scurry along the ceiling while maintaining his distrust.

"And he's friendly?"

"Friendly-ish," Alex replied. "I raised him from a pup."

"Does he know where he's going?"

"He's tracking Holt and Damon," she informed him. "He'll alert us to danger."

They approached a streak of blood, alarming Bundy. "A creature killed one of the guys there," he informed her. "Do you suppose they ate him?"

"Monster isn't much of a meat eater," she remarked. "Mostly spiders and clams. He prefers mangos." She looked around while sinking into thought. "Seems strange that his relatives would be meat eaters."

"So, uh, how do you know Damon?" Bundy asked while eying her. "He never mentioned a woman out there. Just some old guy and his son."

"Apparently, I'm the son."

"That son-of-a-bitch," he cried out. "He lied to me. He wanted you for himself."

"You talk a lot."

"Hey, I haven't seen or spoken to a woman in over eight years, and my best friend has been keeping you a secret from me," Bundy groused with little care. He was obviously irritated with his friend. "So, are you two, like, seeing each other?"

She rolled her eyes at the constant questions. It had been years since she'd been around someone so talkative. "I should have left you in the kitchen."

"Ah, that's not a denial," he announced enthusiastically while grinning.

Monster stopped and thumped his tail on the doorframe. Alex held her hand up to silence Bundy. Bundy became alert and concerned. Alex moved into a fighting position and quietly moved closer to Monster near the doorway. Alex cautiously entered the laundry room with her pole leveled. Monster scurried along the ceiling but remained close. Bundy looked around. The laundry room was massive and contained many large washers, dryers, laundry bins, and racks of clean laundry to obscure their view. They heard a commotion within the room. Alex and Bundy headed through the room and stopped. Several men attempted to elude one of the creatures while pinned near the large dryer. One man was dead in a pool of blood, but the creature was holding the rest captive. The creature spun toward Alex and Bundy.

"Oh, shit," Bundy gasped.

One of the men ran while the creature was distracted. The creature leaped on the man, tackled him face first to the floor, and grabbed his neck in its teeth. The creature snapped the man's neck, nearly ripping his head from his body. The five remaining men ran from the scene. The creature released the dead man and spun toward the running men. Alex took her attack stance with her pole. Bundy appeared horrified, but for some reason, he didn't run. The men stopped when they saw Monster on the ceiling.

The creature leaped for Alex. Monster ran across the ceiling and dropped down in front of Alex to protect her. He swung his massive tail for the creature, nailed it in the chest, and tossed it backward with force. The creature struck the dryer and was momentarily dazed. It then leaped to its feet and hissed at Monster. Monster stood on his hind legs and growled loudly. The creature appeared intimidated and ran up the dryer and across the ceiling. Without hesitation, Monster leaped to the ceiling and chased after it.

"We'd better get out of here," Bundy suggested.

The men motioned them to the door. Alex followed the commotion from within the laundry room.

Bundy grabbed her hand. "We need to get out of here in case he doesn't win."

Chapter Thirty-seven

Bundy and Alex followed the five remaining men into the nearby cellblock, which was apparently where the group of over thirty inmates had spent the last few years. The overnight attack seemed to have thinned their pack drastically. It was difficult to say how many had survived. One of the men shut the cell door and locked it with an old key. Everyone finally relaxed, feeling safe for the first time. Alex looked around the dismal cellblock. It was as dark, drab, and depressing as the rest of the prison. At least there were outside windows, obviously covered with bars, which allowed sunlight to enter the cellblock. Alex finally got a better look at the five men she and Bundy had met within the laundry room.

Dan and Marv were fairly large men in their late thirties. Although their clothes were slightly dirty and wrinkled, they kept better care with their hygiene. They remained unshaved for a few days but had bathed recently. They typically kept their hair buzzed close to their heads, but it appeared as if they were in need of another buzz. They were neither good-looking nor homely.

"We'll be safe in here," Kyle informed them. "They can't get into the cellblock."

Kyle was a strange looking man and came across as high-strung. Although he seemed to take care of himself, and his clothes were relatively clean, he had a slightly creepy look about him. Alex didn't like the look in his eyes or the way he looked at her as if she were an appetizer.

"What the hell were you guys doing in the laundry room in the first place?" Bundy demanded.

"We hadn't heard anything in a while," Garrett responded while recovering from his ordeal. "We thought we could make it to the kitchen. Starving to death wasn't really an option either."

Garrett was a big, tall man in his early thirties. He stood over six-foot-four with enough weight behind him to do some damage. He was a powerhouse of a man. He had moderately short, dark hair, which he kept neat. Possibly considered a good-looking man, he didn't seem to be a very intelligent man. The men had a difficult time keeping their eyes off Alex. She remained near the main cell door and watched for Monster. When he appeared outside the door, the remaining men jumped with alarm.

"It's okay," Alex informed them. "He's with me."

"Believe it or not, that's her pet," Bundy replied dryly.

"There's no way I'm letting that thing in here with us," Phil insisted.

Phil was the last of the five men from the laundry room. He was average height and build with short, neat hair and a clean-shaved face. He obviously took great care in keeping himself clean and dressed properly. Although ruffled by what had happened over the last two days, Phil seemed to have a better grip on his emotions.

Alex cast a look at Bundy and clutched her pole. "We have to go," she announced sternly. "We need to find Holt and Damon."

Bundy nodded then looked at Kyle. "Unlock the door," he ordered. "We have to find Damon."

"No way man," Kyle protested with fear in his eyes. "That thing is out there."

"That's her pet, Kyle," Bundy snapped with irritation. "It's not going to hurt us. Give me the key."

Kyle eyed Alex with more than a passing interest and barely looked at Bundy. "Where did you find a woman, Bundy?"

He extended his hand, clearly annoyed. "Just give me the key, Kyle. We'll worry about the Q and A later."

Phil finally joined their conversation while grinning his lustful intentions. "We're all stuck here. We may as well make the best of it," he announced then gave Alex a lengthy once-over. "What's your name, honey?"

"Give Bundy the key or I'll wipe that grin right off your face," she snarled.

Garrett laughed while looking at the other men. "She's a feisty one. I like them feisty." He moved closer to Alex and grinned. "Why don't you come to my cell and you can show me just how feisty you are?"

"Really, Garrett?" Bundy snapped while glaring his irritation. "You haven't seen a woman in eight years, and you're going to be a total pervert?"

"Goes way beyond pervert, Bundy," Kyle informed him, revealing his full, creepy potential.

Phil grabbed Bundy from behind while chuckling.

Bundy attempted to break free. "Let me go, or I'll kill all of you!"

The remaining four men grinned at Alex and circled her. Alex eyed them with little emotion. She casually twirled her pole above her head and moved into attack position. She watched the four men out of the corner of her eyes without turning her head. Monster snarled from the cell door. His tail cracked like a bullwhip, causing the man near the door to jump. The others easily ignored the angry creature.

"Oh, look at her," Kyle teased. "She's sexy when she's acting all tough."

Bundy fought against the man holding him immobile. "I'm warning you! Stay away from her!"

"He's warning us," Kyle remarked and laughed. He glared at Bundy. "Sorry, buddy, but I'd assume kill you and keep the girl. She's what we've been missing on this rock."

Alex remained still while watching the four men surrounding her. Two of the four attempted to grab her from behind. Alex spun with the pole, cracked each man, and spun back in time to strike the remaining two. The men cried out with each strike from the pole but didn't appear dissuaded. Bundy broke Phil's hold and fought him with the same Navy SEAL training Damon had displayed on the beach. Phil didn't stand a chance. Bundy snapped Phil's neck and dropped him to the floor. As he turned to Alex, she beat all four men, keeping them at bay. One was already writhing around the floor while clutching his head. Bundy stopped to watch her with surprise and amazement. As Marv flew Bundy's way, Bundy grabbed him and snapped his neck without hesitation.

While Alex pummeled two of the three men, Bundy fought Garrett and wasted little time ramming his head into one of the cell doors. He fell to the floor, apparently dead. Alex continued her assault on Kyle and Dan. Dan had enough and attempted to flee. Bundy struck him in the throat. Dan was thrown backward from the impact and spit up a large amount of blood as he hit the floor. He twitched and no longer moved. Alex finally took down

Kyle with her pole and several karate kicks. He lay on the floor gasping and holding his hands in the air.

"No more. I give," he cried out. "You win."

Alex backed away and maintained her emotionless expression, allowing Kyle to stand. Bundy kicked Kyle in the groin. As he doubled over, Bundy snapped his neck. Alex stared at him with the same shocked expression she'd given Damon.

"Was that necessary?"

Bundy glared at her and pointed a demanding finger. "Do you have any concept of what they intended to do to you?"

"Yes, and I handled it."

"But I handled it better," he snapped then appeared curious and shook his head. "Why didn't you take them down with a groin shot?"

"I'm not supposed to fight dirty."

"Not supposed to fight dirty? Do you want to live?" he demanded. "Is Damon going soft on me?"

"I didn't learn from Damon."

"Obviously," Bundy muttered. "Does he know you can fight like that?"

"Yes, I pinned him five for five."

Bundy suddenly chuckled. "Oh, yeah. He definitely wants you for himself." He removed the key from Kyle's pocket. "Let's go find the prick. I don't want some creature killing him before I have the chance."

Chapter Thirty-eight

Damon and Holt entered the library which contained high bookcases filling the large room. It wasn't the most modern library nor the most glamorous, but it contained thousands of books both fiction and non-fiction. Holt stared at the shelves and shelves of books and marveled as they crossed the room.

"I think I just died and went to heaven," Holt practically gasped.

"Be in heaven later," Damon scoffed then looked around, carefully checking the dark corners. "I can't believe we haven't found anyone."

Holt eyed several titles on the shelves as they passed. "Judging by all of the blood we've found, I don't think we're going to either," he remarked.

"Bundy has to be alive," Damon remarked. "He's about as crafty as they come."

Holt suddenly stopped and eyed Damon with a curious look on his face. "Is this the same scene you found when you arrived on the ship?"

"Unfortunately, yes, but I don't understand why we haven't seen any creatures in all these years," he remarked while shaking his head. "Did they find a nice spot to hibernate for the last eight years?"

"Since no bodies were found, it's possible they took them to their nesting spot and fed off them then hibernated," Holt informed him. "Another scenario could be cannibalism. Like a queen bee. They bring her a nest full of food, and she kills them."

"That's gratitude, huh?"

"Nature can be cruel," Holt announced with a defeated sigh.

They heard a low gurgle instantly forcing both men to freeze in their tracks. They uncertainly looked around the nearby shelves. A creature lurked on top of the bookcase not far from them, staring at them while flashing its sharp teeth.

"Oh, shit," Damon gasped.

"Don't move," Holt whispered. "It'll leap on you before you can get out of its path."

Damon clutched his machete without taking his eyes off the creature. "Don't move?" he gasped in a whisper. "Will standing here do any good?"

"From what I've observed with Monster, don't look it in the eyes," he informed him. "You don't want to show aggression."

"I don't think that's going to work," Damon muttered without moving and finally took his eyes off the creature to glare at Holt. "It wants us dead."

"I can't defeat it by hand or with my pole," Holt firmly insisted. "Alex play fights Monster, and she's never won."

Neither man moved and kept from making eye contact. The creature crawled down the bookcase and approached Holt. Holt remained still. The creature sniffed him and snorted then moved away from Holt to check out Damon. Damon remained still and avoided eye contact. The creature rose to its hind legs and stood taller than Damon. Damon tensed and clutched his machete.

"Don't--" Holt scolded under his breath.

The creature bared its sharp teeth and hissed in a chilling manner. Damon thrust his machete for the creature. It whipped its tail for Damon, knocking him to the floor. The creature was about to leap on Damon when Monster dropped down between them and roared. Damon rolled out of the creature's path. Monster and the creature lunged for each other, rolled across the floor, and crashed into the bookcase near Holt. Holt leaped out of the way and joined Damon.

"That's Monster," Holt gasped while watching the creature. "Please tell me Alex--"

"Are you okay?" Alex called out to them from across the room.

Bundy was directly behind her as she approached them. Holt stared at her with horror and possible anger.

"Damn it, Alex--" Holt cried out.

"We need to get out of here," Damon shouted.

They heard a sharp wail and looked at the fighting creatures. Monster moved away from the dead creature and ran to Holt. Holt cried out as Monster leaped on him and tackled him to the floor. Monster licked his face then jumped off him.

Holt groaned and slowly stood while gingerly rubbing his sore body. He looked at Alex and turned angry.

"You were supposed to stay outside," Holt lashed out at her.

"That's the fifth one he's killed," she informed him while completely ignoring the comment. "There's no telling how many of them are running around this place. We should leave."

Damon and Bundy exchanged manly hugs, happy the other was alive.

"What's to stop them from following us?" Bundy questioned.

"We need to destroy them," Holt insisted.

"How? We couldn't even fight off one without Monster," Damon demanded and daringly raised his brows. "If he's out numbered, he won't survive either."

"Most of them must be female," Alex informed them. "The females kill the males after mating."

"How do you--?" Damon began.

"Did Monster breed with one?" Holt interrupted with a look of surprise.

"Yeah, and then she immediately tried to kill him," Alex replied.

"It could be they come out to breed, collect food, and then go into hiding to lay their eggs," Holt remarked while sinking into thought.

"Who said anything about eggs?" Damon suddenly demanded.

"I did--just now. I assure you; they come from eggs," Holt informed him. "One must kill the others and take control of the nest. If we can find that nest, we can destroy it."

"Do you honestly think they'll let us near it?" Damon demanded while shaking his head in disbelief.

"We need to figure out their gestation cycle. If I'm correct, they'll only be active for a few days then return to the nest," Holt informed them. "Once there, the others will be killed leaving just one. The nest will be in a confined space. We can make some Molotov cocktails and burn them."

"That sounds just crazy enough to work," Bundy remarked as a strange, tiny grin crossed his face.

Damon shook his head at his friend. "You're just itching to blow up something, aren't you?" He then looked at Holt. "Supposing you're right; how do we know when their rampage ends and they return to the nest?" Damon asked.

"I need to dissect one," Holt announced then indicated the dead creature. "That one will do. Where's the infirmary?"

Chapter Thirty-nine

Alex joined Damon and Bundy in the infirmary, which was little more than a glorified nurse's office with some added medical supplies and machines that more than likely didn't work. They watched Holt dissect the large creature on the metal table. He already had the creature spread open, exposing all its internal organs. All three cringed while watching Holt up to his elbows in entrails. Monster hung from the nearby wall and watched with great interest. Holt seemed to be enjoying his exploratory surgery a little too much. He now looked more like a mad scientist than an archeologist.

Bundy eyed Damon several times before finally speaking. "So exactly when did you intend to tell me about your girlfriend?"

Damon didn't bother looking at him. "Never."

"Some friend you are."

"I didn't want to kill you if you drooled over her," Damon snarled.

"Hey, I've never tried to steal a girl from you," Bundy announced defensively.

"You're right, you didn't," Damon remarked. "You also never let me get to them first."

Alex moved closer to them while listening in on their conversation. "Are you two talking about me?"

"Just guy talk," Damon informed her.

"He's afraid I might woo you away from him," Bundy teased.

"I'm not looking to trade-in Damon," she casually informed him. "Holt is starting to warm up to him, and I'm pretty sure he wouldn't like you at all. You talk too much."

Damon grinned. "See, she's keeping me."

"I can't imagine why," Bundy scoffed.

"Apart from him being very handsome," she announced boldly, "I'm told there's a fifty percent chance I could be pregnant."

Damon and Bundy looked at Alex with shared surprise by the announcement.

"He told you that?" Damon gasped.

"Yeah, he's not particularly happy with you, but I did hear him humming "Rock-a-by-baby"," she teased.

"How many mangos is that in child support?" Bundy joked with Damon.

Damon smacked Bundy on the shoulder, causing his friend to flinch and gingerly rub his arm.

"Owe, that hurt."

Damon stared at Alex with some surprise. "Why didn't you say something?"

"Fifty percent isn't yes or no," she informed him then appeared curious. "Are you upset?"

"No, of course I'm not upset," he assured her. "I'm sure Holt could read a book and have childbirth down to a science in one night. I just don't want any complications that we can't handle."

Bundy snickered while mocking his friend. "Damon's gonna be a daddy."

Damon backhanded Bundy in the groin with just enough force to make him gasp.

"She's right," Bundy gasped while gingerly rubbing his crotch. "I do talk too much."

"Amazing!" Holt suddenly cried out.

All three approached Holt and the dissected creature on the table.

"She's already carrying developed eggs," Holt proclaimed. "They've grown very fast."

"Does that help us?" Damon asked.

"Absolutely," Holt announced cheerfully. "They're probably going to return to their nest within twenty-four hours. If I'm correct, within thirty-six hours, there should only be one female left."

"How will we find the nest?" Damon asked.

"Monster will find it," Holt insisted. "Decaying bodies, creature eggs, and a female? He'll be able to locate that nest with no problem."

"So we just hole up here until tomorrow evening?" Bundy asked then turned enthusiastic. "I'm all for that." He then eyed Monster. "How long can he go before we become appetizing to him?"

"Monster isn't a meat eater," Alex insisted.

"His sisters apparently are," Bundy muttered.

The following day, the kitchen appeared quiet and empty, although there was blood covering the floor and the walls. The dead creature and all the human remains were gone, leaving little more than blood strewn everywhere. It was a gruesome scene not unlike the one Damon discovered when he arrived on the boat and found the prison abandoned years ago. Damon made an announcement over the intercom instructing everyone to gather in the kitchen. Alex remained in a far corner with Monster while waiting for the survivors. Holt, Damon, and Bundy stayed near the kitchen entrance, eager to see who had survived the attack. To their surprise, Miller and Tyler, who had been hiding in the pantry, were the only survivors.

"Is this all of us?" Damon asked with surprise.

Miller and Tyler kept close watch on Monster in the corner where he happily ate mangoes next to Alex. Despite being reassured he was safe, they remained cautious.

"Everyone else is dead," Miller finally informed them. "You're sure the threat has been neutralized?"

"More like dormant," Holt remarked. "There's a small matter of containment."

"Containment?" Tyler questioned with concern. "What does that mean?"

"If Holt is correct," Damon announced, "in three days' time, the alpha female will kill all the creatures. She'll protect hundreds of eggs capable of bringing about more creatures when conditions are right."

"So why haven't we seen these things before?" Miller asked.

"Conditions weren't right," Holt replied. "The eggs remain dormant for years. Apparently, the environment was right for hatching the eggs just as it had been the year you arrived and found the prison abandoned."

"How was it possible we didn't have this sort of outbreak six years ago?" Alex asked. "Was Monster the only egg to hatch?"

"Monster was possibly washed out of the nesting ground where his egg found the right environment to hatch," Holt replied. "That's my best guess."

"So what do we do?" Tyler asked.

"We find the nest and destroy the eggs," Damon informed him.

Chapter Forty

Three days later. Alex, Damon, and Holt followed Monster into the basement, while Bundy and the remaining two men toted homemade explosives behind them. The basement was a large area of organized clutter. Surprisingly, the basement looked better than most of the prison areas.

"I've been down here," Damon insisted. "I would have seen eggs or a nest."

Monster stopped by the back wall near the storage area. There was a small opening close to the floor that was barely noticeable. Damon stared at the small opening, surprised a creature could even fit through there.

"Oh, you've got to be kidding," Damon gasped. "There's no telling what's beyond that."

"Seriously, we can't go through there," Bundy replied in response.

Alex turned to Monster and stared into his eyes. "We need to find the outside entrance, Monster."

"Alex," Holt announced with a sigh, "I know Monster is smart, but he--"

Monster scurried along the ceiling.

"He's smarter than you think," she informed him.

Damon turned to Miller and Tyler. "You two stay behind and seal up that hole," he ordered. "We don't want any escapes this way."

Miller and Tyler nodded and stayed behind. The others followed Monster.

§

Monster led them deep into the woods beyond the prison grounds. At first, it seemed as if they were being led in circles. They finally came to a clearing where there was a small cave opening near the stream.

"That's it," Holt announced with enthusiasm. "This stream would probably flood high enough to have washed Monster out as a pup."

Damon lit torches for Bundy and himself. Alex and Holt entered with Damon just behind Monster. The four stopped fifty yards into the cave. Monster remained still and quiet. The cavern was filled with stalagmites and stalactites of varying sizes. The environment was cool and damp, although the area became warmer as it widened. There were hundreds of eggs within the cavern.

Not far from the area filled with eggs was a pile of old bones containing hundreds of bodies nearly a decade old. Not far from the bones was a pile of decaying human remains. The piled bodies were obviously the recently killed prisoners. They were to be meals for the hatching creatures and their mother. As Alex and the men scanned the cavern, they finally saw the lone female sleeping among the eggs. She suddenly woke, hissed, and ran along the ceiling toward them. Monster snarled and leaped for her. They clashed and fought. Teeth snapped, claws slashed, and tails cracked. Bundy appeared eager to light his homemade explosive.

"No, we wait until Monster is safe," Damon firmly instructed his friend.

The large creatures battled violently. Alex held her breath, concerned for Monster. Obviously, this female was the strongest to have killed all the remaining females. Alex wasn't sure Monster could defeat the alpha female. Both creatures sank their teeth into the others tough exterior while clawing at their more vulnerable underbellies. Monster whipped his tail, cracking the female with harsh blows until she finally released him with her teeth.

The alpha female cracked him with her tail and sent him across the cave, destroying several dozen eggs along the way. She lunged for Monster, who seemed slow returning to his feet. Alex held her breath and stared with fear in her eyes. Monster wailed loudly, whipped his tail, and caught the female across the face. She was thrown backward with force and struck one of the stalagmites, breaking it. She fell to the cavern floor and immediately sprang to her feet for a return assault. Monster leaped on top of her, grabbed her by the neck, and shook her violently until her neck snapped.

"Now?" Bundy cried out.

Monster sniffed the nearby eggs. All eyes were on the creature. He cracked one open with his front claws as if opening a clam and ate the gooey, egg-like substance.

Bundy's expression dropped, and he grimaced. "Okay, that's just disgusting."

"That's why the females kill their mates," Holt announced with realization. "Males destroy the eggs."

"Aren't we going to burn them?" Bundy demanded.

"Actually, we should just let Monster deal with it in his own way," Holt replied with a sigh.

Chapter Forty-one

They waited outside of the cave for nearly half an hour. Monster finally appeared from the opening in a hurry and jumped into the trees. They immediately lost sight of him.

"We'd better check his handy work," Bundy announced. "Make sure they're all destroyed."

Bundy and Holt entered the cave while Alex looked around the trees for Monster.

"Is everything okay?" Damon asked her.

"Yeah, I just thought Monster would be bloated and tired from his omelet buffet," she announced. "I don't see him."

"He's probably up there somewhere sleeping it off," Damon remarked. He hesitated then offered a pleasant smile. "Given who's left alive here, I was thinking you and

Holt should move into the prison. It's not much, but we have indoor plumbing and plenty of room."

"Well, as long as Holt agrees to it," Alex replied.

"Oh, he'll practically live in the library," Damon informed her while grinning. "I want us to be together. Not an entire island apart." He pulled Alex into his arms. "Monster can have his choice of cells."

"And the other prisoners?"

"None with history of violence against women or children," Damon happily replied.

"I'll trust you." She heard movement in the trees. "Oh, there he is. I'll catch up with you then."

Alex hurried after Monster, surprised how fast he was moving considering how bloated he must have been after his feast. Alex entered a small clearing and looked around. Monster climbed down a tree and approached her. Alex was about to speak then stared with surprise. He had a baby creature in his mouth. It wailed softly. Monster placed it on the ground near her feet and pushed it toward her. Alex eyed the baby creature and uncertainly lowered herself to it. She eyed Monster with surprise.

"You spared this one? Why?" she questioned. "Did you want to keep it?"

Monster gurgled.

She studied him a moment. "You want me to raise her to be like you?"

Monster again gurgled. Alex picked up the creature, held it in her arms, then eyed him and sighed.

"She'll need to be sterilized, so she doesn't produce any eggs when she's old enough."

Monster wailed softly in response.

"Yes, you're right. We don't want her trying to kill you after mating too." Alex stared at the baby creature and sighed deeply. "Holt's going to be cranky about this," she insisted while eyeing Monster. "You'd better be extra nice to him if we're to win him over."

Monster gurgled and nuzzled the baby creature in Alex's arms.

§

Six months later. The cleared prison yard had an impressive garden where the overgrown vegetation once overran the yard. In a neatly cleared exercise area, Holt taught Damon karate moves. Alex and Damon practiced together and appeared very comfortable with each other. Bundy played basketball with Miller and Tyler on the basketball court. Monster suddenly jumped from the fence into the yard. The female creature leaped on top of him. They rolled around then stopped and nuzzled each other.

The End

Other books by Holly Copella!
Reviews left on Amazon are appreciated!

"The Battle for Andrea Maria"

A cruise ship attack turns six survivors into overnight celebrities after they take credit for the heroic act of a stowaway who died saving them.

The cruise is just what Jess needed--a bit of harmless fun far from her daily grind. But what begins as a relaxing vacation turns into a desperate fight for her life when terrorists take over the ship and start piling up bodies. Teaming up with a mysterious stowaway, Jess attempts to send out a distress call but knows they cannot wait for help to come. If she or the few remaining passengers have any hope for survival, Jess must act now. The papers dub it "The Battle for *Andrea Maria*," but to Jess it is the moment she fought side-by-side with her enigmatic Romeo, saving the ship--and losing him. She thinks the story ends there, but really, the nightmare is just beginning...

"Insanely Deadly"

When the dead return to life, it's up to an admiral's daughter and a mildly insane, former war hero to save their small town.

Jetta Cross, a Navy Admiral's daughter, is tasked with keeping her father's comrade, a former war hero turned town crazy, grounded in the real world. Capt. John Hunter is still fighting the war in his head, where imaginary dead people are part of his world. When a viral outbreak brings about a zombie uprising, Hunter is left to his own devices. He must resume his role as a one-man commando unit in order to destroy the ravenous undead. With Hunter still fighting his own inner demons as well as the undead, the townspeople fear their zombie neighbors may not be the only threat. Stranded at the island's luxurious resort with a handful of workers, Jetta is forced to live up to her father's reputation and take charge of the deteriorating situation at the hotel. She must wage her own war against the infected before the government declares her hometown a total loss.

"Deadly Institution"

A town recluse suspected of killing his wife teams up with a young woman in order to stop a killer.

After being accused of murdering his wife, Konrad Asher turns his back on the town that once adored him. Ten years later, he still holds his grudge and the title of the most feared man in town. With the reopening of the burned mental institution, where his wife had died, former employees are now murdered one-by-one, throwing suspicion back on Asher. A young local reporter, Jacey, is forced to reveal her long-time friendship with the infamous recluse in order to clear his name not only in the recent murders but to exonerate him in the death of his wife as well. Will Jacey's relationship with Asher invite the killer closer to her? Or is the killer already in her life?

"Screenplays: The Island Collection"
"Jungle Princess", "A.L.F. Resort", "Brighton Island"

Discover how romance and fun in the sun can be downright *chilling*!

"Jungle Princess" is a romantic/thriller that leaves a teenage girl stranded on an island with two male shipmates and a creature of "unknown" origin. She soon discovers the island is home to an abandoned prison with several prisoners roaming free. What really killed over one hundred prisoners? And is it still out there--?

"A.L.F. Resort" is a romantic/thriller set on an island resort with Artificial Life Forms as the main draw. At this resort, all your fantasies come true...until a malfunction removes safety inhibitors on the A.L.F.'s. Zombies, biker gangs, and mobsters run amuck, turning fantasies into nightmares. A young reporter gets more of a story than she anticipates, but will she survive long enough to write the story?

"Brighton Island" is a romantic/thriller set on a private island. When the owner's niece brings her psychic friend to the mansion, his presence awakens the spirits' tortured souls. As the psychic attempts to solve the old murders, the niece is confronted with the possibility that she's next to join the mansion ghosts. Stranded on the island with a crazed killer, her uncle wages his own war to save them. Will his "shock and awe" tactics actually save them or get them killed?

"Death Displacement"

A grief-stricken man travels back in time to seek revenge on the woman who murdered his girlfriend but inadvertently falls in love with her.

Kane is about to marry the woman he loves. His life is perfect. A few weeks before the wedding, a vindictive woman from his girlfriend's past mysteriously arrives and kills her. He learns of a traumatic accident that happened five years earlier, which triggers Riley's hatred for his girlfriend. Distraught over his girlfriend's death, Kane uses an antique time machine to travel into the past in order to find and destroy the woman responsible. When he runs into Riley's younger self, he realizes she's not the monster she later becomes, and he can't bring himself to destroy her. With a little help from his oddball friend from the past, they formulate a plan to prevent the accident that sends Riley down her destructive path. Kane's plan backfires when he falls for the younger Riley. His new tortured existence is further complicated when future Riley, his girlfriend's killer, shows up with her own devious agenda that doesn't include him. Will he be able to stop the time ripple, which ultimately ends with his girlfriend's death? Or will future Riley take him out of the timeline forever--

"Dead Village"

After strange happenings isolate a small resort town from the rest of the world, nearly one hundred residents seek refuge at the closed hotel. Only eight survive the night. And that's just the beginning...

One day after the entire population of Fox Ridge Village disappears, a car wreck forces several unsuspecting crash victims to seek help at the closed summer hotel. Within the hotel, they discover the grisly aftermath of a brutal slaughter. Crash victims Vander and Devon, a reluctant clairvoyant, team up to solve the riddle of the "haunted hotel" and the mass hysteria plaguing the remaining survivors. By the time they discover the hotel's secret, they're already drawn into the hysteria. As the body count continues to climb, it's a race to isolate the source and bring everyone back to reality before they kill one another. Will Devon be able to communicate with the traumatized spirits before their fate becomes her own?

"Misfits, Inc."

A seemingly ordinary, young woman meets four misfits who claim she has given them supernatural powers.

While on a business trip to a remote island paradise, a bored secretary, Hailey, has her world turned upside down when her path collides with a psychic freak, Skyler. He attempts to convince her that they had met in his dreams, and she had chosen him as one of her four mystic warriors. After Skyler foresees a woman's death, they discover an unidentified creature has killed one of the guests. They are joined by a lounge pianist and a rich playboy, who also claim they had met her in their dreams. If Skyler's prophecies are genuine, the evil entity controlling the ravenous creatures needs to destroy Hailey to ensure its survival. Reluctantly accepting her fate, Hailey has to locate the last and most powerful of her chosen warriors, The Guardian. Their fate is in doubt when The Guardian turns out to be a self-absorbed, former cat burglar with a bad attitude. Can Hailey turn her company of misfits into an elite team of mystic warriors? Or will The Guardian's secret agenda destroy them all?

"Basement Dwellers"

A viral outbreak at a hospital leaves a mortician, sheriff, and coroner fighting for their lives against a horde of undead and the CDC.

After a massive car wreck leaves several survivors in critical condition at the local hospital, a surgeon uses experimental drugs on his critical patients and accidentally causes a zombie outbreak. When local mortician, Lexx, receives an infected corpse as her client, she becomes stranded in the hospital basement during CDC quarantine along with the local sheriff and the coroner. The infamous surgeon struggles to find a cure for his infectious blunder by using the other survivors as test subjects. Meanwhile, Lexx and the sheriff attempt to locate his missing sister, who's stranded somewhere in the battle zone that once was the emergency room. It's a race against time and the ravenous undead. Can they survive the undead before CDC sanitizes the hospital of all infection?

"Witness Protection"
Also available in audiobook!

After witnessing an execution, a resourceful young woman attempts to disappear while being pursued by a hitman and a handsome federal agent.

A helicopter pilot, Jackie Remus, reluctantly agrees to go on a date with one of her clients, but her date is unexpectedly cut short when she witnesses a man being murdered. After narrowly escaping with her life, she is placed into protective custody. When the safe house is breached, Jackie makes a daring escape from both the hired killers and the handsome FBI agent, who wants to return her to protective custody. With a little help from her sly and crafty friend, Monroe, Jackie is convinced she can disappear until the trial. While on her journey to meet with her friend, she solicits help from a few shady but lovable characters along the way. Although she manages to stay one-step ahead of the hired killers, the federal agent remains in hot pursuit. Will Jackie reach Monroe before she's captured by the FBI and returned to protective custody? Or will the hired killers silence her first?

"Town Darling"

After surviving a brutal attack that claims the lives of those she loves, a young woman seeks revenge on a corrupt town.

Going back home is never easy, but for Casey, it means returning to her corrupt hometown where she barely survived a brutal attack. Accompanied by two family friends, she seeks justice for the night that destroyed her life. Her physical scars are nothing compared to her emotional ones, forcing the local sheriff to believe that the town darling is back for revenge. As the conspiracy for her revenge appears to be leading up to the coveted town fair, the sheriff is determined to stop her from fulfilling her vengeful scheme...but guilt over his role on that fateful night continues to haunt him. Will his desperate need for Casey's forgiveness be his undoing? Or will Casey's desire for revenge destroy them both?

"Unconditional"

A young woman puts her life on hold to care for an unstable, highly skilled combat soldier, who believes someone is trying to kill him.

A botched military coup leaves a team of elite fighters injured with one clinging to life in a coma. When Harlan wakes from his coma, he's left with no memory of his past life. His commander's daughter, Indy, takes it upon herself to care for the fallen war hero. She's challenged with more than just his physical care as she combats with not only his memory loss but also his newly found desire for her. His infatuation with her becomes the least of her worries when he sinks back into his role of a combat soldier. Believing his life is in danger, his fighting skills surface, turning him into an unpredictable and dangerous man. Will his memory return to him before Indy is forced to commit him? Or will he finally find his nemesis, "the coyote", and possibly claim the life of an innocent person?

"Witness Protection 2"
The Return of Whiskey Tango Foxtrot

Believing she holds the clue to millions in missing laundered money, a young woman is placed into the protective care of a former Navy SEAL team.

Feeling sorry for her recently separated co-worker, Leeann invites Wiley to join her and her friends on their night out. Little does she know that finding her co-worker murdered is just the beginning of her nightmare. Leeann unknowingly holds the key to fifty million dollars in potentially laundered mob money. With hired killers pursuing her, the FBI places her into a different kind of protective custody. Former Navy SEAL team Whiskey Tango Foxtrot reunites to keep Leeann alive at their secret hideaway. What should be an easy assignment takes an unscheduled turn when secrets, lies, and betrayal threaten to derail their mission. Is the team prepared for a war on their own doorstep? Will Leeann's misguided trust endanger the lives of those sent to protect her?

"Deadly Institution 2"

When blackmail turns into murder, a young woman finds herself caught in the killer's crosshairs.

The small town of Stony Ridge is no stranger to scandal and persecution of the innocent. When a brutal killing shakes the town's prestigious country club, Jacey McMurray seeks help from a self-proclaimed vigilante, Konrad Asher. As her professional and personal worlds collide, Jacey fears the stress of the country club killings have finally taken their toll on Asher. Can a stressed out vigilante stop the killer before he strikes again?

"Witness Protection 3"
Alpha Mike Foxtrot

A helicopter pilot risks her life to help a team of retired Navy SEALs rescue two girls from a killer.

When former Navy SEAL team Whiskey Tango Foxtrot asks for a simple favor, Jackie reluctantly offers her air-taxi services. What could go wrong? What begins as a search and rescue for two girls turns into a fight for survival against a heavily armed drug cartel. Wanted by the law with the cartel in hot pursuit and their home base breached, the team is forced to call in a favor from a questionable ally. Unfortunately, their new safe house isn't what it seems. Without knowing who the real enemy is, can Jackie and the team save their young witnesses from the hands of a killer?

"The Pen Pal"

In order to save her friend, she must enter the mind of a serial killer.

When her best friend is abducted, no one believes Jolynn saw it in a psychic vision. With nowhere to turn, Jolynn reluctantly joins Agent Harris Slade and his team on their hunt for a sadistic serial killer known only as "The Pen Pal". Finally confronted with the killer, Jolynn realizes she must enter the mind of the psychopath in order to stop the brutal killings. But when her vision reveals a particularly disturbing death, can Jolynn sacrifice her lover for her friend?

"Awaken the Dead"

A grieving innkeeper struggles to keep her haunted hotel out of foreclosure.

After losing her parents in a suspicious boating accident, Harley Brandon is determined to keep the family hotel out of foreclosure. Unfortunately, the hotel ghosts have other plans. Built with tainted money, the century old Horizon Hotel thrives on a tradition of murder, scandal, and suicide. As the paranormal activity increases to alarming levels, Harley discovers the truth about the hotel and its residents. Can Harley save her friends from the hotel's frightening hidden secrets?

"Already Dead"
Supernatural Collection

From the already dead to the undead. Three supernatural tales of "things that go bump in the night".

"Bloodletting" - A vampire themed resort allows guests to *participate* in their Bloodletting Ritual to celebrate the island's legendary vampires.

"Reaper of Souls" - A young woman must outwit an evil sorcerer in order to save her brother or become one of his minions forever.

"Already Dead" - When Flight 220 crashes, ten passengers make it to an isolated island, but only one man lives to tell the lie.

"Witness Protection 4"
O-Dark-Hundred

A simple assignment turns deadly when a retired Navy SEAL team uncovers a plot to kill a notorious mob boss.

When Whiskey Tango Foxtrot embarks on a simple stalking case, they're not prepared for a trip to a private island paradise owned by an infamous mobster. With one of their own suffering from traumatic head injuries, the team is left scrambling to decide what is real or imagined. The situation escalates even further when they uncover an assassination plot where everyone is a suspect. Now targets themselves, can the team survive their trip to paradise?

"Witness Protection 5"
Outside the Wire

After suffering several casualties on their last assignment, a retired Navy SEAL team discovers their misery is just beginning.

When Whiskey Tango Foxtrot returns home after suffering a devastating loss, they're hit with even more bad news regarding the rest of their team. Their grief is cut short when they discover their names are all on the same hit list. Hunted by relentless assassins, the scattered team must decide whether to remain safely hidden or find the man who put the price on their heads. Against the wishes of her teammates, Jackie strikes out on her own in order to save a friend who wants her dead. In a kill or be killed situation, will Jackie's emotions finally betray her?

"Once Upon a Disaster"

A young homicide detective finds herself at the mercy of a hitman in the aftermath of an earthquake

While investigating the murder of a hitman, Detective Jade Wesson pursues a lead connecting the dead man to a break-in at a computer programming company. She's drawn into the world of nightclub owner and front man for the mob, Cody Riley. Her investigation keeps pointing to Cody's right-hand man and possible hitman, Vahn Lott. Despite her efforts to keep her investigation on track, Vahn has plans of his own for the attractive detective. When an unprecedented earthquake rocks their east coast town, Jade must put her life in Vahn's hands if she wants to survive. Can she trust a man who might be the killer she's hunting?

"The Murder of Emily Fisher"

After finding their favorite teacher murdered, the lives of two teenage girls are forever changed.

Everyone loved Emily Fisher. While walking home one afternoon, two teenage girls, Sidney and Trisha, stumble upon a gruesome murder scene. The brutal murder of Emily Fisher, a young, attractive schoolteacher, shocks the small town of **Marilina**. After graduation, Sidney moves far away from the memories of the small town while Trisha retreats deeper into denial. Eight years after the murder, Sidney receives a desperate call from her childhood friend, forcing her to return home. Trisha believes Emily's killer was falsely accused and she manages to turn the entire town against her while attempting to prove it. When Trisha receives a death threat, Sidney realizes there may be some credibility to her friend's wild accusations. Is Trisha's mental breakdown a result of childhood trauma? Or is the real killer actually attempting to silence her? In order to save her friend, Sidney must answer the eight-year-old question. Who murdered Emily Fisher?

"Castle Bloodshed"
Murder Collection

From a deadly island paradise to haunted castles. Three novella length tales of murder, mystery, and malicious intent.

"Castle Bloodshed" — A tour of Wesley Castle turns into a fight for survival as six stranded tourists discover the haunting secrets within the castle walls. A mystery writer teams up with an uptight butler in order stop a killer who may already be dead. Novella length paranormal murder mystery.

"Fleshies" — Is Uncle Rutger crazy? Five years ago, four business partners died within their newly purchased, fixer-upper castle. Their bodies were never found. The surviving partner, Rutger, claims a demon keeps him as its slave. Rutger's nephew schemes to save his uncle by sacrificing the lives of a group of stranded motorists and a high-profile novelist. Novella length supernatural murder mystery.

"Demon Island" — A group of strangers are invited to a remote island for the reading of a will. The guests soon discover they were brought to the island to be executed one-by-one. It's up to a private detective and a tenacious young woman to solve the murders and find a way to escape paradise. Novella length murder mystery.

"Brighton Island"

When a psychic visits a haunted island mansion, he inadvertently awakens the ghosts' tortured souls.

Something's not right with Simon. When Jacklyn brings her eccentric friend to her uncle's island mansion, she didn't expect him to slip into psychic overload. As Simon attempts to solve a decade-old, double homicide, Jacklyn is confronted with the possibility that she could be next to join the mansion ghosts. When they find themselves stranded on the secluded island, her Uncle Hyland wages his own war to save them from a flesh and blood killer. Will her uncle's "shock and awe" military tactics save them or get them killed? Can Simon bring peace to the tortured souls or unexpectedly join them?

201

"A.L.F. Resort"

A fantasy vacation turns into a nightmare when the resort's artificial life forms are compromised.

Welcome to A.L.F. Resort where you can live out your fantasies with safe, state-of-the-art artificial life form robots! When a young journalist and a photographer are sent to A.L.F. Resort to do a story for their magazine, Shay and Becka believe they've hit the jackpot of all work-cations. The engineers pull out all the stops to make their fantasies memorable. Unfortunately, the newly designed A.L.F., the Gen X, is smarter than his programming and creates havoc within Shay's fantasy. A computer malfunction removes their safety inhibitors and the A.L.F.s play out their own hostile fantasies. Zombies, bikers, and mobsters run amuck, turning fantasies into nightmares. Shay gets more of a story than she anticipates, but will she survive long enough to write it?

Coming Soon!
"Witness Protection 6"

ABOUT THE AUTHOR

Holly Copella has been writing since the age of twelve when her frustration at a book's poor plot drove her to author her own story. Over the last decade, she's written a number of screenplays, some of which she's now adapting into novels. Her fascination with zombies and other darker material lends an edge to her writing, which tends to lean toward horror. As a fan of Agatha Christie, she appreciates the craft of a good plot and the importance of creating significant characters.

Hailing from Pennsylvania, Copella lives in the Endless Mountains on a farm with her rescue horses and other animals. In addition to writing and reading fiction, she enjoys riding horses and traveling to Las Vegas and Disney World.